Axis Stone Mysteries

THE ZIGGY STARDUST DEAD RINGER

G. L. Keady

Published in Australia in 2024
by Big Island Publishing

Big Island Publishing
PO Box 3027, Tuross Head, 2537, NSW, Australia.
www.bigislandpublishing.au

ISBN:
E-book: 978097633007
Print: 9780975633038

Edited by: Canon Doyle
Cover design and art: Brandon Evans-Keady

TABLE OF CONTENTS

CHAPTER
ONE

In Nashville, Tennessee, a city synonymous with country music and its rich historical legacy, the music scene is fiercely competitive. Known as the mecca of country music, Nashville has been instrumental in shaping the careers of many prominent artists. Amidst this vibrant backdrop, 'The Local' stands out as a popular venue, showcasing live acts most nights and drawing in a crowd keen on discovering fresh talent.

Into this dynamic environment stepped a mysterious solo artist, an enigma who seemed to have appeared from nowhere. Unmanaged and unsigned, this artist was a rarity in a city where almost every musician is vying for recognition and representation.

This solo artist auditioned at 'The Local' and remarkably secured a regular late Friday night spot. This accomplishment was no small feat in Nashville, where securing stage time at a renowned venue like 'The Local' is a dream for many. Here, talent is abundant, and every corner of the city teems with artists yearning for their big break.

The success of this solo artist in such a competitive landscape was a testament to their unique talent and appeal. The artist had managed to stand out in a city where standing out is both essential and incredibly challenging. The music and persona sparked intrigue and conversation, not just within 'The Local' but across Nashville's bustling music scene.

Word of this solo artist spread rapidly, igniting curiosity among music lovers and fellow musicians alike. Questions about his identity, background, and the distinctiveness of his music became a frequent topic of discussion. In a city like Nashville, to capture the audience's heart and curiosity in such a manner is a remarkable achievement, highlighting the singular talent and charisma of this mysterious solo performer.

This artist, unmanaged and unsigned, was a whisper of intrigue in a city where every melody seeks an ear, and every singer yearns for a spotlight. Nashville, a crucible of musical dreams, had found in its midst a performer who defied the usual narrative.

At 'The Local', where the neon lights flicker promises of fame and the wooden stage echoes with history, this solo artist earned a regular late Friday night spot. In Nashville, where the air itself seems laced with tunes and every street corner is a stage, this was no mean feat. It was a coveted slot in a city where music is the lifeblood and competition is as fierce as the southern sun.

This artist's ascent to a regular spot at 'The Local' spoke volumes. In a city bursting at the seams with talent, to stand out is a feat akin to finding a rare melody in a symphony.

Who was this solitary figure whose tunes captivated the crowds? In a city that prides itself on knowing the backstory of every strum and lyric, this artist was an alluring enigma, a mystery unfolding on the stage of 'The Local.'

If I was to refer to this artist in the masculine, it could certainly be a mistake, as nobody knew the true gender of the performer. Androgynous might be the most fitting descriptor. This mystery only added to the intrigue that enveloped them in Nashville's bustling music scene. Performing at 'The Local', a venue that resonated with the city's rich musical heritage, this artist drew an audience composed solely of women, a phenomenon as curious as the artist's ambiguous identity.

The appeal of the artist wasn't just in the unusual music and compelling performance. Much of the fascination stemmed from the striking resemblance to David Bowie's iconic character from the early

1970s, Ziggy Stardust—a hermaphroditic figure that Bowie had immortalised on stage. This likeness led to speculation and whispers among the crowds. Some even ventured to suggest that this performer was not merely emulating Bowie's Ziggy Stardust but was the actual alien being Bowie had portrayed: a messenger who came to Earth bearing hope and ultimately revered as a prophet.

To many, it seemed that Ziggy Stardust was being reborn, achieving a similar cult status that Bowie's character once held. This growing phenomenon began to cause concern, especially among parents whose daughters were drawn to the enigmatic artist. One such parent was Sheriff Tanner, who watched with unease as his own teenage daughter became captivated by this mysterious figure.

In a city like Nashville, where music legends are born and fade, this new, otherworldly presence on the stage of 'The Local' was carving a unique niche. The artist's androgynous allure and the mystery surrounding his identity were not just a topic of conversation but a burgeoning cultural phenomenon, creating ripples that extended far beyond the confines of the music venue.

The transformation in these girls, once they became fans of the androgynous artist at 'The Local', was striking. Their personalities and dress codes underwent a noticeable shift, mirroring the ethos of 60s/70s hippies. Flowing garments, vibrant colours, and a newfound sense of freedom in their expression became the norm among these teenage women. It was as if they were channelling the spirit of a bygone era, one that spoke of peace, love, and liberation.

To Sheriff Tanner, this was more than just a trend. Watching his Ivy League-educated daughter morph into a modern-day hippie was deeply unsettling. To him, it echoed a darker chapter in history—a 21st Century echo of the Manson family. The thought that this transformation could spiral into something as terrifying and uncontrollable was enough to send alarm bells ringing in his mind.

Furthermore, the Sheriff had his own image and reputation to consider. In his view, the influence of this LGBTQIA+ performer, with his enigmatic presence and ability to sway the youth, posed a threat to the social order he was accustomed to. He was not prepared to let this performer, regardless of his popularity or talent, compromise the values he stood by.

The situation was rapidly evolving into something more than just a musical phenomenon; it was becoming a cultural and social conundrum. Sheriff Tanner, feeling the pressure of his position and personal beliefs, saw it as imperative to step in and curtail what he perceived as a growing threat. The challenge, however, lay in how to approach this without escalating tensions or infringing upon the freedoms that were so deeply ingrained in the city's ethos.ß

~ ~ ~

Charlie had an enquiry of a musical nature, more aligned with my expertise than his. Thus, over a phone call, he sought my opinion. A friend had reached out to him about a performer in Nashville who was being targeted by the local law enforcement. Knowing my stance against any form of persecution, Charlie correctly assumed I would be interested.

Until then, it had been a conventional witch-hunt, until the artist was accused of murder. Charlie briefed me on the details.

"The artist's name is Ziggy Stardust."

"Wait a sec, isn't that a David Bowie alter ego?"

"Yes, but this individual claims to actually be that persona."

"Interesting … go on."

"Ziggy has become quite a draw in Nashville, but peculiarly only for young women. Once they become fans, they undergo a transformation."

"In what way?"

"They start emulating hippies from the 60s and early 70s, complete with all the associated styles. Not all of them, but enough to raise concerns among parents and the like."

"Is this due to Ziggy's philosophy or something?" I queried.

"No one seems certain … he doesn't appear to be preaching in his songs … but he owns a small ranch just outside Nashville, to which these girls are drawn, eventually living there in a sort of hippie commune."

"Sounds reminiscent of Manson," I observed.

"That was the initial worry among local law enforcement. However, when the Sheriff's daughter ended up as one of the flock, things escalated."

"I can see why that would happen. Go on, mate."

"First, Ziggy was assaulted, an incident he didn't report to the police. However, the Sheriff's daughter did, implicating her father."

"Naturally."

"Then, when a young girl disappeared and was later found brutally mutilated near his ranch, Ziggy was arrested on suspicion of murder."

"So, what are they asking of you?" I inquired.

"The Sheriff's daughter reached out to a friend of mine, requesting me to investigate the murder. The Sheriff's office has closed the case, charging Ziggy with murder. However, she insists she and a couple of friends were with Ziggy at the ranch at the time of the murder. Moreover, she's adamant that Ziggy is vehemently against any form of violence."

"What's your take, Charlie?"

"It won't pay the bills, but I feel a moral duty to represent the underdog."

"We're carving out a niche for representing the LGBTQIA+ community," I noted.

"That's not a negative, is it?"

"Certainly not. A nice diversion from the usual triads ... Okay, let your friend know I'll take the case. Have them send a contract from your office and ask Carol to forward me one of Ziggy's songs. Oh, and could you get Enzo to conduct a background check on him?"

"No problem. Will you be coming here, or heading straight to Nashville?"

~ ~ ~

I was greeted at Nashville International Airport by Brian X, the eccentric and technocratic friend of Charlie's. His long hair, beard, jeans, and Pink Floyd T-shirt marked him as my kind of guy. Stepping outside, the dry 32-degree Celsius heat struck me like a left hook. As my armpits began to betray me, we located his immaculate 1970 orange and white VW Kombi, complete with perfectly functioning air conditioning.

I had asked Trish to book me into the Conrad Hotel in downtown Nashville. En route, I inquired about Brian's background.

"I started out as a recording engineer here in the early eighties," he explained, "but it wasn't long before the new digital era made me redundant."

"I thought studios were making a comeback?"

"That's true, man, but I've been out of that loop for too long now."

"So, what did you do?" I asked.

"I mixed live gigs, then got a day job at Bridge Audio, designing home theatre systems. I still moonlight mixing gigs, but I'm picky about the music."

"Country?"

"Hell no, that's on every corner here. I'm into progressive rock."

"Like Floyd?"

"The T-shirt's a dead giveaway, huh?"

"Hey, I'm a fan. My folks were too; my dad even met them."

"Far out."

"So, is that how you met Ziggy?" I probed.

"Sure did. I've been doing Ziggy's front-of-house since day one."

"So, tell me about Ziggy."

For the next 15 minutes, Brian provided a comprehensive overview of Ziggy's character and music. From his account, Ziggy Stardust was as, if not more, enigmatic than David Bowie. Firstly, he appeared out of nowhere; secondly, his music emanated from a mysterious forty-centimetre square black box with a line in and an optical stereo out, running on its own phantom power. The most outlandish thing? He never used a microphone, yet his voice carried to almost any sized auditorium. I mentioned I'd listened to the track 'Walrus Dreams' and thought it was excellent. He agreed.

"I recorded it for him, you know how?"

"No."

"Directly out of that black box into a digital recorder."

"What about the vocal and the harmonies?"

"This is the thing ... the black box records every gig, processes it, and spits out a beautifully mixed-mastered audio file, harmonies and all."

"That's bizarre," I said, genuinely astounded, especially considering Brian was a qualified audio engineer.

"I tell you, if I knew how that black box worked, I'd be richer than Elon Musk."

"Could Ziggy have murdered Wendy Ram?"

"No way, man. I've never met anyone more peaceful and chill than Ziggy ... wouldn't hurt a fly. Wendy's old man is Cyrus Ram, into nightclubs and car dealerships, one of the richest dudes in Tennessee, worth around 4 billion and running for governor. One tough mother he is, has a whole lot of influence with the big end of town."

Brian pulled up in the forecourt of the Conrad.

"Man, Ziggy will die in the big house if you can't get him out. He's way too fragile."

"You think he's screwing the girls at his ranch?"

"No way man, doesn't seem to me he partakes in sex of any kind."

I got out.

"Thanks for the lift, Brian."

"Happy to run y'all 'round if needed."

"How about we meet up in Thistle and Rye bar at say 6? I should know a bit more by then."

~ ~ ~

Enzo Cipriani, Charlie's key investigator, was ushered into Charlie's office by the receptionist, Carol. Enzo harbours a crush on Carol but, despite his tough biker persona with the Mongols, he's shy around women he's attracted to. Charlie and Carmen, both aware of his feelings, often encourage him to ask Carol out. Carol, sending Enzo every conceivable signal of interest, which he invariably fails to recognise, leaves him with Charlie and Carmen.

"I sent Axis the lowdown on Ziggy Stardust," Enzo began, settling into a seat in the lounge area of the office. "Not much to find, though. The guy's a mystery—no passport, no birth certificate, no employment or IRS records, not even a police file. I can't fathom how someone gets by in this day and age without credit cards, a driver's license, and all the other shit."

"Nor can I," Carmen replied, astounded.

"You mentioned you ran into Serina Sun?" Charlie inquired.

"Yeah, I was in the vegetable section at Ralphs on La Brea and saw her picking out a cucumber. Made some smart-aleck remark about it, and she laughed. Then, realising who I was, she unloaded about being robbed, not once, but twice … and the cops did squat about it."

"When were these robberies?" Carmen interjected.

"Last week and the one before. At her house, not a hold-up or anything, while she was on set."

"What was stolen?"

"That's the odd thing—nothing."

"Nothing? Then how does she know she was robbed?" Charlie chuckled.

"The security footage. She showed me on her phone. A burglar, fully decked out, breaks in, disables the alarm, then twenty minutes later reactivates it and leaves."

"So he knows the pin … Does the footage show the burglar elsewhere in the house?"

"No, just both sides of the front door and the alarm control panel in the foyer."

"He's either searching for something he hasn't found yet, or he's a crazed fan."

"Or a sexual deviant, getting off on her lingerie," Carmen speculated.

That got an odd look from both men.

"So, um, she wants to hire us to catch the burglar. Said the studio will foot the bill; they don't want her stressed during the shoot," Enzo rasped.

"A good chance to network with the studio," Carmen advised, "There's plenty of straightforward, lucrative work with them."

"Particularly with Pegasus, they're the big gun in town right now," Enzo declared, with evident enthusiasm.

Charlie rose from his wicker chair and fetched three beers from the bar fridge. As he distributed them, he remarked, "Okay, let's draft a contract for Pegasus. Enzo, would you mind briefing Carol?"

As Enzo exited the room, beer in hand, to see Carol at reception, Carmen whispered to Charlie, "Matchmaker."

Charlie grinned, and they clinked bottles in a toast.

~ ~ ~

I settled back in my room at the Conrad, poring over the file Enzo had given me. Impossibly, there was absolutely nothing to go on. In these times, everyone had a trail—IRS, driver's licence, credit cards—something. But with this person, there was nothing; it was hard to believe. How does this guy live? I wondered. The house phone rang, and I anticipated a return call from the police department.

"Hello, yes, speaking. Ah, thank you for calling. I'd like to speak with the detective in charge of the Wendy Ram murder case. Yes, I'm a private investigator. No, I'm not at liberty to disclose my client. Okay, Detective Chris Miller, thank you. I'll see him then."

The Metropolitan Police Department was just a five-minute walk from the Conrad. Opting to walk, I soon regretted the decision, wishing I had taken a taxi to avoid arriving in a wet shirt. The CID was on the 4th floor. After a brief search, I located Detective Miller's office and knocked on the door. The detective, with a thin face, wore a crumpled brown suit, a beige shirt, and a bolo tie. His penetrating gaze met mine from behind his desk.

"You must be Stone. Take a seat," he said with a Tennessee twang.

"Detective, I'm retained to investigate the murder of Wendy Ram," I began.

"I'll stop you right there, Stone. We have the murderer; the case is closed." His tone was eerily cold, and his obvious eagerness to dismiss me left me feeling uneasy.

"Well, sir, my client disagrees and has the right to hire a private detective to investigate."

His eyes narrowed, regarding me as impertinent, before he snarled, "You'll get no assistance from me. Will that be all?"

"I guess it will. Are you always this hospitable, Detective, or is it my aftershave?" I asked facetiously.

He peered at his computer monitor, dismissing me with a curt, "Good day, Mr Stone."

Well, that went well, I mused, exiting the building. I was on my own, but at least Ziggy had the right to apply for bail. Heading towards the Municipal Court, just three blocks away, I planned to speak with the court clerk.

CHAPTER
TWO

The meeting with the court clerk was as brief as the one with Detective Miller; it seemed to me that everyone in Nashville was intent on pinning the crime on Ziggy Stardust. Bail had been denied, but I at least obtained the name of the defence attorney. Deciding to speak with him before visiting Ziggy's ranch and interviewing the commune members, I headed to Clifton, Reece & Weiss attorneys at law on Church Street.

Upon entering, I approached the reception and inquired if I could speak with David Reece, Ziggy Stardust's defence lawyer. The middle-aged receptionist, her brown hair styled in a beehive reminiscent of the band the B52s, regarded me with a look reserved for expired yogurt in a supermarket. After gesturing for me to take a seat, she periodically cast sly glances at me over her 1950s style cat-eye glasses.

Ten minutes later, she signalled for me to proceed through a door. Inside, an open plan office buzzed with activity, and a dapper-looking gentleman in his sixties greeted me with an outstretched hand. Introducing himself in a Tennessee drawl as David Reece, he led me to his office, which offered a distant view of the Cumberland River in downtown Nashville. Reece's pleasant demeanour was a welcome change. After a brief introduction about myself and the purpose of my visit, we delved into the details.

"Ziggy is remanded in custody, charged with first-degree murder, and bail has been denied."

"What evidence is there?" I inquired.

"From what I've gathered, the evidence is scant. Ziggy was the last person seen with Wendy Ram alive on the night of the murder. Would you like a copy of the police report?"

"Thank you, that would be helpful."

"Look, I'll be frank with you, Stone. Wendy Ram comes from one of Nashville's most prominent families. Her father, Cyrus Ram, wields significant political influence; he's running for governor. Since Ziggy began attracting young women to his commune, he has irked some powerful figures in the community."

"Like Sheriff Tanner?"

"Yes, and others. You have to understand, these girls represent the flower of Nashville's youth. In the Sheriff's case, his daughter was an Ivy Leaguer, cheerleader, school captain— the epitome of Nashville society. And she abandoned it all to live like a hippie with Ziggy Stardust. It's not difficult to see why the community turned against him. Sherri Tanner is just one of a dozen of Nashville's finest now lost to what resembles a Charles Manson-like hippie commune."

"So a charge is trumped up to rid the community of he who begs to be different … sounds like the plot of a 1950s western movie. So, Mr Reece, are you in harmony with the community chorus?"

His response was a look of guilt.

"I see. Can you arrange me a visit?"

"Yes, when would you like?"

"By what I've uncovered since arriving this morning, as soon as possible please, before he's lynched."

Reece chuckled macabrely as he picked up the phone to make the arrangements.

Walking out of the law offices, I made my way towards the Downtown Detention Center, located a few blocks south, opposite Public Square Park. By the time I reached the stark Sheriff's Office Downtown Campus, my shirt was soaked through with sweat.

The process of entry was smoother than I anticipated, likely a result of Attorney Reece's legal clout. A stoic officer guided me to an interview room. The blast of air conditioning was a welcome relief from the sweltering heat outside.

A short while later, the unmistakable sound of chains and the rattle of a door handle signalled his arrival. The door opened to reveal Ziggy Stardust. His appearance was startling: dressed in standard orange prison attire, he was about 6' 2", exceedingly thin, with striking red hair, devoid of eyebrows, and sharp facial features set in a triangular face. His resemblance to David Bowie's Ziggy Stardust was uncanny. Androgynous, he moved with a fluid, almost feminine grace. The guard secured his handcuffs to the table, then left us alone.

"Hello, Ziggy. My name is Axis Stone, a private detective. Miss Sherri Tanner has retained me to investigate the charges against you."

"A rare few offer support. Please, call me Eo," he replied, his voice carrying a musical quality that seemed to resonate within my mind.

"Thank you, Eo. Why the name Ziggy Stardust?"

"The character suited me."

"I see. Where are you from, Eo?"

"That is complicated. Right now, proving my innocence is what matters. I will not survive long in here."

His concern echoed the fear of incarceration that I knew was a significant issue among Indigenous Australians.

"Are you in danger from inmates or guards?"

"No, I just cannot be contained."

"Okay, you knew the victim Wendy Ram?"

"Yes."

"Can you recount the night of the alleged murder?"

"Of course. I performed at The Local as usual. Afterward, we left for my ranch."

"No time backstage, no dressing room?"

"I do not dwell at the venue. Sherri was driving, Wendy Ram and Chaka Zuma were on the back seat."

Eo described a chilling scene on a dark, secluded road. Ziggy sat meditating in the passenger seat of the grey Chevrolet Bolt EUV.

Sherri, young and blonde, was at the wheel. Wendy, with vibrant red hair and pale skin, laughed in the back seat, joined by Chaka, an African-American beauty. The three girls were wearing white caftans and no make-up.

Bright headlights suddenly flooded the car interior. The approaching car, aggressive and fast, began to tailgate them. Sherri veered towards the shoulder to allow the car to pass. It started to pass but remained parallel with them, then it suddenly swerved towards them, forcing them off the road into a rough, skidding stop, that threw them about inside the car.

Shaken, Sherri asked, "Are you guys okay?"

"It nearly hit us," Chaka gasped in panic.

The taillights of the menacing car suddenly lit up, and it began reversing towards them. "They're coming back," Sherri said, her voice laced with fear.

The car stopped mere inches from the Bolt's grill, effectively trapping them. A man emerged from the driver's side, his form silhouetted against the headlight's glare. He walked purposefully toward them.

"Who is it?" Wendy asked, her voice trembling with fear.

"I can't make out his face, but he's carrying something ... looks like a gun," Sherri whispered, her voice barely audible.

As Sherri was about to hit the central door locks, the man reached their car. He was wearing a macabre plastic mask, grotesque and doll-like, which obscured his face. In one swift, violent motion, he yanked open the rear door and grabbed Wendy, pulling her out of the car as she screamed in terror.

His movements were swift and brutal. He dragged Wendy, who was kicking and struggling, to his car. He opened the front passenger-side door and shoved her in, her cries muffled by the closed door. The man then got back into the driver's seat, performed a U-turn, and sped off into the darkness.

Inside the Bolt, a stunned silence enveloped us. Sherri sat frozen, hands still gripping the steering wheel, her eyes wide in shock. Chaka was sobbing quietly in the back seat, her body shaking. We sat there, terrified and speechless, the echoes of Wendy's screams still ringing in our ears.

Eo's recounting of the event was calm, but the stark horror of that night was palpable in his every word. "That is how it happened," he concluded, his voice a mere whisper in the now eerily quiet room.

"Did you phone the police?"

"Sherri phoned her father, he is the Sheriff."

"And what resulted from her call?"

"Nothing."

~ ~ ~

Charlie and Enzo, having reviewed CCTV footage from Serina Sun's old house, deduced that both burglaries occurred while Serina was on set filming 'Woman of the Night.' The time stamps indicated 9 pm for both incidents, suggesting someone knew her shooting schedule. With another shoot scheduled for the same time that night, they decided on a stake-out.

Charlie waited in his car outside the old house on Woodland Lane in Laurel Canyon, while Enzo stayed concealed inside. It was Enzo's first stake-out, whereas Charlie, more experienced, had often conducted surveillance from his car, typically observing unfaithful spouses through binoculars.

Enzo checked his phone; it was exactly 9 pm. He braced himself for action.

As if on schedule, the front door creaked open. A dark figure slipped inside, headed straight for the alarm control unit, and opened it. Suddenly, a torchlight flickered on, illuminating the burglar's face. Startled, the burglar froze, then dashed towards the partly open front door, only to be confronted by Charlie on the other side.

Enzo pressed the barrel of his Glock into the burglar's back and growled, "Hands up!"

Charlie removed the burglar's balaclava, revealing a shock of blonde hair. The burglar was female.

"Let's go inside and talk about what you're doing here," Charlie suggested.

They escorted her back inside, turned on a light and settled in the living room.

"Okay, talk," Charlie demanded.

"Are you cops?" she asked.

"Listen, cat woman, we're the ones asking questions here," Enzo said firmly. "Who are you, and why have you been breaking into this house?"

She appeared to be in her early thirties, attractive, and not fitting the typical burglar profile they had expected.

"I'm on a job," she said, "I'm a private detective."

~ ~ ~

I was draining a glass of vintage JD in the Thistle and Rye bar at the Conrad when I saw Brian enter. He appeared better dressed than before, likely influenced by the Conrad's ambiance. I ordered him a JD, and we found a table where I briefed him on my progress.

"He's an odd sort of person, what do you know of him?"

"Very little, I met him when I was mixing another act at The Local—it was Ziggy's first gig..."

"You mean his first gig in Nashville or first ever?"

"Well, as you probably know, he doesn't talk much. I asked him where he'd previously played, and he said that's complicated."

"Yes, he told me the same when I asked where he's from."

"Right. And there's something else. Nobody has ever seen him eat. Sherri, who's been living at the ranch commune, confirmed it."

"That's bizarre. What does he live on, air?"

Brian leaned forward, lowering his voice. "And there's more. The song 'Walrus Dreams' that I sent you, it's about being in London in the 70s. The lyrics, 'Yesterday, so far away, I hear the streets of London say, you're a long way, such a long way, from home ... strawberry fields, feel so real, and Walrus dreams, on village greens, seem a long time, such a long time ago,' suggest he was there during the Beatles era. This would mean he's in his 70s now."

"But he looks barely in his early 20s," I noted.

"Exactly, but here's the thing," he took out a small notepad to refer to. "I used a sound spectrum analyser on 'Walrus Dreams' and found unusual frequencies in the song. One is 111 hertz, which releases endorphins in the brain to calm people, you know ... and, and, what's even more freaky is the other frequency is subliminal at 852 hertz, which is referred to as the 'Love Frequency,' one of the Solfeggio frequencies ... Solfeggio frequencies have a repeating pattern of six codes according to sound therapists. On the basis of these six codes, the frequencies can be reduced to the cross sums 3, 6, and 9. Nikola Tesla is supposed to have regarded these three numbers as code numbers of the divine, a Fibonacci sequence; the creative power and the energy of the physical fields. To each of these frequencies, a syllable is assigned. The origin of the ancient Solfeggio scale can be traced back to a medieval hymn to John the Baptist. The hymn's first six lines of music each began on the first six consecutive notes of the scale, and thus the first syllable of each line was sung one note higher than the first syllable of the previous line. Since the music had a mathematical resonance, the original frequencies were apparently capable of inspiring humanity and being 'closer to God.' When I looked further, I found all nine of the original main Solfeggio frequencies in the song... healing frequencies, man."

"Is this a Buddhist thing?"

"Yes, similar tones are used in Tibetan monk chants."

"And these frequencies are subliminal?"

"Yes, that's what's extraordinary, man."

I really liked the way Brian thought—many would call it eccentricity, but to me, it was sheer genius. I sat back in my seat, deep in thought. "So, you think Ziggy ... who told me his real name is E o... is sending messages of peace and love subliminally in his music ... and that maybe that's what's attracting his young female disciples?"

"Told me to call him Eo as well. But, hey, yes, that's why the idea of him killing Wendy is way out of the ballpark, man, it's just not in his nature."

"But still, seventy plus years old, a black box that delivers his music and mixes it complete with ancient subliminal healing frequencies—what the hell are we dealing with here?"

CHAPTER
THREE

"So, Miss Gerri Jewel, private detective, please explain why you've been breaking into Serina Sun's home?" Charlie asked.

"My client believes an item of importance to him is hidden in the house."

Enzo, sceptical, queried, "Who's your client?"

"You know I can't disclose that," Gerri replied curtly.

Enzo was aware of the protocol but thought it worth a try. "So, what is this item?"

"I can't tell you that either."

Charlie was unimpressed. "So, you're basically not going to tell us anything."

"You know the code, Mr Chan. I'll tell you this much: this house is a rental, built in 1959 and sold in 1960 to a famous actor. He had a British butler who came from previous employment in Hong Kong and lived in the attic. My client believes the butler had brought something from Hong Kong that possibly led to his murder."

"Murdered? Here in this house?" Enzo interjected.

"Yes, in the attic. He was found hogtied, in a pool of blood, his throat slit. The incident shocked the owner and generated such controversy that he left Hollywood."

"Was the murderer ever found?" Enzo probed.

"No."

"Was the owner suspected?"

"No. He was in Europe at the time, and left the house vacant until he died in 1993. It was then inherited by his daughter who lived in London and had no interest in the property. The house changed hands several times until it recently became a rental. Miss Sun has been renting it for the past six months."

"Why did your client wait so long to start searching for this item?" Charlie asked.

"My client is a screenwriter. He stumbled upon the item's existence during research for a script."

"And finding it is crucial to the plot of his screenplay, I presume?" Charlie surmised.

Gerri nodded, impressed by Charlie's deduction. "Correct."

"Well, we represent Miss Sun. I suggest you discuss this with your client, so we can arrange for you to legally search for this 'item,' Miss Jewel," Charlie concluded.

~ ~ ~

After expressing my desire to visit Eo's ranch, Brian offered to drive me. On the way, he insisted we stop at Grillshack Fries and Burgers in East Nashville, claiming they had the best burgers in town. He was right.

The journey to Hickory Trail Drive took about thirty minutes. The dark, wooded road was exactly as Eo had described it—the perfect location for an abduction due to its isolation and the scarcity of vehicles.

Brian navigated the driveway weaving through the woods towards the homestead. "How much would a property like this cost, Brian?" I asked.

"Eo paid four hundred thousand for it. In cash."

"Cash?" I echoed, surprised.

"Yeah. He had no credit rating or bank account, so he bought it in my name, then later transferred it to one of the girls, I think Sherri."

"So he started the commune after buying the ranch?"

"Seems like it. The commune wasn't planned; it just happened. He bought the place not long after his first gig."

"So he already had the cash?"

"Yeah, sure did."

We pulled up at the two-storey mountain chalet. "Quite a place for one person," I remarked.

"It's got a lot of bedrooms," Brian replied as we got out.

Approaching the house, the porch lights greeted us. The front door swung open, revealing a blonde woman in a caftan.

"Hey Sherri," Brian greeted. "This is..."

"Axis Stone. We were expecting you. I thought you might come straight here," Sherri said, welcoming us. "We've prepared a room for you. Please, come in."

Inside, she led us to a living room with a large wood-burning fireplace and an extensive leather lounge. Two more girls, Chaka Zuma and Chrissy Liu, joined us.

"I initially met with the defence attorney and Eo," I explained.

"How is he?" Sherri asked, concern in her voice.

"Hard to read. He doesn't show much emotion."

"He's always calm," Chaka commented.

"I've never seen him angry or upset, even when arrested," added Chrissy, a slender, attractive Asian girl.

"He was arrested here?" I inquired.

"Yes, that's when I contacted your partner. Brian gave me the contact," Sherri explained.

I asked the others to leave so I could talk to Chaka privately about the night of Wendy's murder. Her story matched Eo's almost verbatim.

I interviewed Sherri alone next. Her account was more distressed than Chaka's, likely due to her being the driver and feeling responsible, but it aligned closely with the others.

"Eo said you called your father to solicit his help."

"Yes," she said, sniffling, tears in her azure blue eyes.

"Was that from your cellphone?"

"No, it was agreed among us to discard our cellphones. I called him from the landline once we got to the ranch," she said with a strong Tennessee twang.

"How long after the attack was that?"

"Five minutes? Less than ten."

"And what happened?"

"I'd woken him up, he was angry. When I told him what had happened, he just said, 'you had it coming,' and hung up on me."

"When did the police come?"

"9 am the next morning, and they arrested Eo. We still don't know why. That's why I found Mr Chan through Brian and called him. Eo has nothing to do with this, Mr Stone. It's all about revenge."

"Revenge? What do you think happened to Wendy?"

"I think the guy in the mask was Cowboy, Wendy's last boyfriend. She'd split up with him to join us, and Cowboy wasn't too happy about that."

"How do you know?"

"The Friday before, at The Local, Cowboy came in drunk with three of his buddies and caused a scene. Security had to throw them out. When Eo finished and we were leaving, they were waiting for us outside, drunk as skunks. Wendy and Cowboy had a terrible row, and she slapped him. In front of his buddies, that riled him up big time. We were lucky to get away from him that night."

"So Cowboy set an ambush for the following Friday after the gig?"

"I think so. I don't think he planned on killing Wendy, just hijacking her. I think maybe that turned into a full-on fight; she could be wild and wouldn't take a backward step. He probably hit her, and she knocked her head or something ... an accident. He wouldn't have murdered her."

"What's his real name?"

"Travis Norton, he's the singer of the country rock band, The Haybale Rollers."

"That's some name ... Do you believe Eo is being persecuted?"

"Sure do, by the boys and men like my father and Wendy's dad. They all want him run out of town.

By the time I returned to the Conrad, it was nearing midnight. Too late to call Trish, I was about to step into the shower when I noticed an envelope on the bureau, marked from Clifton, Reece & Weiss Attorneys at Law. I had forgotten that David Reece had promised me the police report on the murder. After a quick shower, I settled into bed to read the report.

The details in the report seemed to align with Sherri's version of events. Wendy had died from blunt force trauma to the head. Her body was found on the side of the road, about a kilometre from the turn-off to Hickory Trail Drive. The report described bruises consistent with a fall and restraint, including discoloration on both wrists, bruises on her knees, and skinned elbows and palms. There was no evidence of rape or forced sexual activity. The key piece of evidence implicating Eo was strands of hair found clutched in the victim's left hand, which perfectly matched Eo's. Beyond this, there was no other evidence.

The findings seemed flimsy to me. It was entirely feasible that the hair could have been planted post-mortem. Without seeing the body myself, the injuries described appeared consistent with someone who had either jumped or been pushed from a moving vehicle.

~ ~ ~

Charlie, having taken a swim and a shower, was dressed for work. As part of his daily routine, he was enjoying breakfast by the pool. He'd prepared his own meal and was now savouring a freshly brewed coffee. Carmen, wearing sunglasses and a canary yellow A-line dress that accentuated her figure and legs, joined him with her coffee in hand. She sat down opposite him under the large blue and white striped umbrella.

"I didn't hear you come in last night, hon," Carmen said.

"I tried not to disturb you; it was after midnight."

"How did it go with Enzo? Did you catch the thief?"

"Actually, yes, we did. One Miss Gerri Jewel, believe it or not. And she's a private detective."

"Are you serious? The cat burglar was a woman, and a private detective? That's unbelievable."

"She was hired to break in and search the house for something."

"What exactly?"

Charlie recounted the events of the previous night. Carmen, though sceptical of Jewel's intentions, was clearly intrigued.

"I wonder what they're looking for?" she asked.

"Maybe we'll find out later today. I've told her to talk to her client so I can get permission from Serina to search."

"Wouldn't the estate agent need to be involved?"

"Only for structural changes, like tearing down a wall or something. I want us to look into the house's first owner. Gerri mentioned he was a famous actor who quit Hollywood after the murder."

"Gerri, huh? So you're on first-name terms?" Carmen remarked, her eyes rolling in a playful yet slightly jealous manner.

Charlie, opting to sidestep her apparent jealousy, simply finished his coffee without comment. He then stood up, signalling he was ready to leave and start his day.

The fifteen-minute drive from Doheny Drive to the office on Sunset was a sombre one, with Carmen harbouring a mood that Charlie couldn't quite understand, or perhaps didn't want to. This unusual mood swing in Carmen was out of character and that concerned him.

Reaching his desk without the confrontation he had anticipated was a relief. Enzo was on his way for a meeting to discuss the case. The phone rang; it was Carol from reception, with Gerri Jewel on the line. Carmen's interest visibly piqued when Charlie mentioned Gerri's name.

"Gerri, good morning. You have? That's great ... yes, ten o'clock works. See you then." He hung up and continued with his work, deliberately avoiding any further discussion with Carmen.

Unable to hold back, Carmen finally asked, "Was that the cat burglar?"

"Yes, she's coming at ten," Charlie replied.

Just then, Enzo arrived in their office, cheerfully pulling up a wicker chair in front of Charlie's desk.

"Morning, everyone," he greeted brightly.

"I just got off the phone with Miss Jewel. She's coming in at ten," Charlie informed him.

Enzo glanced at his watch, noting that it was just twenty minutes away.

"I've got the details on the first owner of the house—it was British actor Stewart Granger. No mention of the murder, but he left Hollywood for Europe in 1967 for some undisclosed reason ... died in 1993," Carmen explained.

"Wasn't Stewart Granger married to Jean Simmons?" Enzo asked.

"Yes, his second wife from 1950 to 1960, one child—a daughter, Tracy Granger. After that, he married the actress Caroline Lecerf in 1964 to 1969, and they had a daughter, Samantha Granger. In all, Granger had four children, all female."

"He was quite the Hollywood luminary, wasn't he? How did he die?" Charlie asked Carmen.

"Certainly, he was. He returned to Santa Monica and sadly died there of prostate and bone cancer in 1993," Carmen said.

"Did Granger leave because of the murder or before it happened?" Enzo inquired.

"From what I've found, he was living in Europe when the murder occurred and chose not to return to that house, but kept it. His daughter sold it after his death," Carmen said.

Charlie was glad Carmen's mood had swung back to normal, that was until the arrival of Gerri Jewel. When Carol brought her in, all three of them were shocked by her appearance—she looked stunning. The sort of beauty that took one's breath away. Both Charlie and Enzo wondered if this was the same cat burglar they'd previously met ... Carmen was boiling with envy.

CHAPTER
FOUR

Charlie and Enzo leapt to their feet to greet Gerri Jewel. "Gerri, great to see you," Charlie exclaimed, ushering her to a seat in the lounge area. Gerri, clutching a yellow briefcase, was attired in a pale blue blazer dress adorned with black double-breasted buttons, showcasing her long, shapely, tanned legs that descended into Stuart Weitzman black suede, ankle-strap, high-heeled sandals. Her attire complemented her shoulder-length, butterscotch blonde hair exquisitely.

Charlie introduced Carmen, and they all settled into their seats.

"My client is willing to collaborate with us as a team, on the condition that you sign a non-disclosure agreement," Gerri stated, her voice deep and husky.

"That would…," Charlie began, but was swiftly interrupted by Carmen.

"It seems illogical that we were employed to safeguard the premises and apprehended you intruding, yet we are the ones to sign a non-disclosure, Miss Jewel," she retorted sharply.

"It's due to the intellectual property involved, Carmen. My client is a seasoned screenwriter, and the item we are searching for is crucial to his current project. He's already secured script development funding from a major studio, hence his caution," Gerri explained, placing her briefcase on her lap, retrieving a document, and passing it to Carmen. "Upon signing the NDA, I can reveal the specifics of the item believed to be in the house."

Carmen examined the document closely, while Carol appeared to take their coffee orders. Satisfied, Carmen handed the document to Charlie, who signed it and returned it to Gerri.

"All set, so...?" Charlie inquired.

"Right, in 1964, the house's owner..."

"Stewart Granger," Carmen interjected.

"Yes, well researched ... Granger imported a British butler from Hong Kong. This butler, Richard Knight, had previously served a wealthy man with a questionable past in Hong Kong. Knight absconded with a map belonging to his employer and took it to Hollywood. This map, purportedly Captain Kidd's treasure map, is believed to pinpoint a hoard worth millions. I could delve into Captain Kidd's entire saga, but in essence, he operated not only in the Caribbean but also from Goa, India, to the South China Sea. His treasure is thought to be buried on an island off North Vietnam's coast. Knight's former employer discovered the map inside an artefact belonging to Kidd, acquired at an auction. Fearing retribution, Knight concealed the map in Granger's residence ... and his concerns were valid. While Granger was in Europe with his new wife, Caroline Lecerf, Knight was tortured and murdered in the house. The motive for his murder remained unknown to Granger and the police, and it wasn't until my client resided in Hong Kong that he learnt of Knight's history from a certain Mr Dubin at the Royal Hong Kong Yacht Club. Knight, a notorious drinker, had once rallied sailors from the club to seek the treasure island but were deterred by a North Vietnamese patrol boat amidst the Vietnam War. In '64/'65, Knight attempted to mount an expedition with film industry associates, masquerading as a film shoot, but presumably, his former employer caught up with him first. Ultimately, the map was never found, and my client firmly believes it remains hidden in the old Granger house."

They absorbed Gerri's tale in silence before Enzo, his tone sceptical, remarked, "That's one helluva story. You sure it's not just part of your screenwriter's wicked imagination?"

With practiced ease, Gerri reopened her briefcase, stowed the NDA, and produced a folder, which she handed to Enzo.

"This folder contains the police report, and forensic photographs of the crime scene and the body."

Enzo, eyebrows raised in astonishment, perused the folder. "Must've taken some serious work to get hold of this."

"It sure did. It had been buried deep to keep the press from getting hold of it. My client spent two years tracking it down."

Carmen, intrigued, leaned in. "Didn't Knight have any relatives or acquaintances worried about his disappearance?"

After skimming the report, Enzo passed it to Charlie, who then handed the 8x10 photos to Carmen.

"No, we found no relatives or friends, except those in Hong Kong who presumed him dead when he vanished after moving to the States. He appears to have been a tormented individual."

Carmen, now engrossed in the report, commented, "He had clearly been brutally tortured. All his fingers were broken ... How can you be certain the murderer didn't locate the map?"

"I guess we can't be entirely certain. As far as we know, no one has reported finding the treasure, and the original owner of the map went to his grave in 1998, never having recovered it."

"Any proof he ordered Knight killed?" Charlie inquired.

"He was a notorious gangster, they called him the 'Big Boss,' or 'the Big Spender.' His real name was Zhang Yan, head of a Hong Kong organized crime syndicate."

"I see, I'm very familiar with triads. Which syndicate, do you know?" Charlie probed further.

Gerri shook her head. "From my research, his wasn't a triad. They were actually in awe of him."

"Okay, I'll look into him through my contacts," Charlie mused, thinking about Zhong, who ran the Hong Kong office and would know all about him. "You say he died in 1998?"

"Yes," Gerri confirmed. "He was convicted of kidnapping and other crimes, sentenced to death, and executed in Guangzhou by a firing squad."

Enzo shook his head and commented gruffly, "Knight can't have been the sharpest tool in the shed to rip off a gangster with that much clout."

"We need to know whether the family of Zhang Yan is still active in the Hong Kong criminal world," Charlie stated.

"Why?" Gerri questioned.

"Because they might want their map back," Charlie said gravely, the weight of his words hanging in the air.

~ ~ ~

I was at the Blue Aster Restaurant in the Conrad for breakfast, waiting for Brian to arrive at 9 am. As I finished my coffee, I contemplated my next move: interviewing Wendy's ex-boyfriend. It was just after 9 when I saw Brian walk in. He sat down, and I ordered him a coffee.

"I did some more analysis of Eo's music last night. Remember those healing tones, the Solfeggio frequencies?" Brian began as he settled in.

"Yes, the ones that correspond to the Chakras," I replied, recalling our earlier discussion.

"Exactly. I told you they're in his music, but last night I discovered something amazing—the healing frequencies are in his vocal."

"Is that because vocals naturally contain a lot of frequencies?"

"That's true, but not all of them. Here's the kicker—I had a recording of him speaking to the audience at The Local, and all those frequencies are present in his normal speaking voice."

"Is that even natural?"

"No, it isn't, and that's what's got me intrigued."

Shifting gears, I mentioned, "I want to have a chat with Cowboy."

"Travis Norton, huh? He's quite the character. His band, the Haybale Rollers, will be playing in town tonight."

"I'd rather not do it before or after a gig."

"Okay. They'll probably rehearse today. I can call my buddy who does front of house for them, find out."

Brian made the call, and we learned that the band would be rehearsing around 2 pm at The Black Dog music room. We planned to arrive at 1:45 pm. Meanwhile, I needed to view Wendy Ram's body. I called defence attorney David Reece, who reluctantly agreed to arrange it through the court with the Davidson County Medical Examiner's Office. But it would take about an hour.

With time to spare, Brian suggested we drop by his recording studio. He wanted to show me firsthand what he'd discovered in Eo's voice.

X Studios was housed in a rundown old shack in downtown Nashville. From the outside, it looked unassuming, but inside, it was a treasure trove of recording equipment. Brian seemed to have collected every piece of second-hand recording junk available, giving the place an eclectic vibe. We navigated through the cluttered space to reach the control room, a stark contrast in its pristine condition. We sat behind the Allen & Heath ZEDi 10FX console as Brian switched on the equipment. The large window in front of us revealed the live room, fully equipped with microphones, a Yamaha baby grand piano, a Pearl drum kit already miked up, and several other instruments. Flanking the window were mounted Genelec monitors. The studio, with its state-of-the-art equipment, despite its outward appearance, must have cost Brian a pretty penny.

I swivelled in the chair to survey the room and noticed a Gibson J40 guitar strung for a left-handed player.

"You a lefty?" I inquired.

"Yeah, man. You too?" Brian responded.

"Yep," I said, reaching for the guitar. "Mind if I...?"

"Go for it," Brian encouraged.

I picked up the guitar and played a few chords, followed by a segment of David Gilmour's solo from 'Comfortably Numb'. Brian listened appreciatively.

"Man, you can play," he said.

I shared a bit of my background with him. "I was in a band back in

Australia, then backpacked to London, joined a band there called 'World'. We recorded a prog rock album, but I couldn't make ends meet. Always regretted not pursuing a career as a muso."

"I'd love to hear that album sometime," Brian said, intrigued.

After putting the Gibson back, Brian focused on the task at hand. He played me the nine Solfeggio frequencies he'd isolated, each sample lasting 30 seconds. The effect was indeed calming. Then, he played the vocals of 'Walrus Dreams' without backing tracks, pointing out the Solfeggio frequencies visible on the spectrum analyser. He did the same with the backing track, where the frequencies were also present. Lastly, he played a recording of Eo speaking to the audience at The Local, revealing the frequencies again in his speaking voice.

"Amazing, man. You're saying this is all natural, not some digital effect?" I asked, amazed.

"Absolutely," Brian affirmed. "The only other places these frequencies occur naturally are in Tibetan monk chants and in nature. Each planet has its own audible rhythm. Earth's is 7.83 Hertz, Mars is 114.72 Hertz, and Venus is 221.23 Hertz. Graham Hancock, ancient civilizations theorist, suggests that ancient civilizations knew all this."

"We're probably only just beginning to understand the extent of ancient advanced civilizations," I mused.

"Yeah, but organized religion often disputes such ideas. Yet, everything in existence is essentially a frequency."

I pondered over Brian's insights. Every statement seemed like a revelation.

"Talking to you is like having a bong," I said with a chuckle.

"Yeah, that's probably why I don't have many friends, too intense."

"Don't worry man, Indian's lived in tents." Brian got my gag and laughed. "So, mate, what does this tell us about Eo?" I asked.

"It suggests he might be an alien, man," Brian speculated.

He wasn't joking. The idea hadn't occurred to me, but now it seemed strangely plausible, especially with the Ziggy Stardust angle.

My phone rang to the tune of 'The Terrible Tango'. It was a brief call from Reece, confirming that I had been granted fifteen minutes to view Wendy Ram's body at 11 am.

"It's 10.30 now," Brian noted. "The Medical Examiner's Office is a fifteen-minute drive from here. We should head out."

Before we left, Brian inquired about my ringtone.

"That's 'The Terrible Tango', a track I wrote and recorded with a friend."

"I love it. It's too good to be just a ringtone. We should do something with it," Brian suggested.

CHAPTER
FIVE

Charlie put down the phone with a bemused expression. Carmen, noticing this from across the room, inquired, "What's the matter, hon?"

"That was Serina. When I told her about the deal with Gerri Jewel, she asked 'what's in it for me?' I wasn't sure how to answer."

Carmen pondered the situation. "She has a point. If there's a treasure and she unknowingly owns the only map to it, she's entitled to a share, isn't she? But maybe it was premature to tell her, considering she hasn't signed an NDA."

Charlie nodded, mulling it over. Just then, his phone rang. "Zhong! Yes, I sent you that email. Hold on, let me put you on speaker." He motioned to Carmen to listen in.

Zhong's voice filled the room. "I was part of the team chasing Zhang Yan back in 1997. We missed out on arresting him. He was captured later by mainland police and jailed in Guangzhou."

"So he wasn't a triad?" Charlie asked.

"No, he was feared by the triads. Zhang Yan had no fear, no conscience, and was very clever," Zhong revealed.

"What about his butler, Richard Knight?" Charlie probed further.

"Not a well-known figure, but the story in your email, it's like an urban legend. The specifics about Knight might be true," Zhong replied.

Enzo walked in at that moment and overheard the conversation.

"Hey Zhong, it's Enzo. Did Zhang Yan's widow end up broke?"

Zhong chuckled. "Another urban myth. Luo Yan left Hong Kong with a hefty fortune. But be cautious with that treasure map. If Luo Yan finds out, she'll want it back. She's as tough as her husband was."

"And the sons?" Enzo prodded.

"Nothing much is known, but if Knight's murder was as brutal as you described, Yan probably ordered it. That shows his influence in LA even back then, so with the sons grown up now, it could be even greater," Zhong surmised.

Charlie thanked Zhong for the insights. "How's everything else going there?" he asked.

"Everything is fine. The club is busy, no issues with the Red Dragon. Haven't had any cases of our own yet, though."

"Don't worry, they'll come. Stay safe," Charlie concluded, ending the call.

He looked at Carmen and Enzo, a serious expression on his face. "So, what do we do about this case? It seems like we're treading into dangerous waters."

Carmen recalled Serina's question. "She asked, 'what's in it for me?'"

"Typical. She's stacking cash from her movie gig and she wants more," Enzo grumbled.

"The lure of treasure can have that effect on people," Carmen remarked.

~ ~ ~

Brian was deep in conversation as he drove us to the Medical Examiner's Office, still fixated on frequencies. "Did you know that frequencies represent colours?" he asked.

"No, I didn't," I replied.

"For instance, A4 at 440 hertz corresponds to orange-red, B4 at 466 hertz to yellow. I have an artist friend who used this concept of 'synesthesia' to paint songs. He did 'Hey Jude' by the Beatles. It was like a musical painting."

"What a trip. Did you see it?"

"Yeah, it was incredible, abstract but fascinating to think it was a representation of a song."

The conversation was engrossing, and I could have discussed it with Brian for days. But my mind kept circling back to Eo and the mystery of how he could naturally produce these frequencies and to what end.

We arrived at the government building, Brian stayed in the car while I went inside. I was directed to offices at the rear of the building, where I was met by Dr Donald Vickerman, the Davidson County chief medical officer. His tall, slender frame and dour expression gave him the air of a mortician. Without much ado, he led me to the morgue, pulled open a stainless-steel door, and slid out a gurney with a body on it, covered by a sheet. He reminded me I had fifteen minutes—the body couldn't be out of the freezer too long without microscopic deterioration starting.

I pulled back the cover. Wendy's good looks had been obliterated. It was always so sad to see someone so young robbed of life. Her chest bore the typical Y-incision of an autopsy. I checked for any post-mortem bruising, but found nothing beyond what was in the examiner's report. The bruises on her elbows and knees, and grazed palms indicated she tried to break a fall. I needed to visit the crime scene.

Half an hour later, we found ourselves standing under the blazing sun at the crime scene. A faint chalked body outline was still visible on the shoulder of the road. I walked us through my theory of what I thought had happened. "This is where she ended up. If the car was heading back towards town and she was in the front seat, as Sherri stated, Wendy should have been on the other side of the road."

"Unless she got up after jumping out of the car and tried to walk back toward Hickory Trail," Brian suggested.

"That's possible," I agreed. "There should be blood from the head wound in the body outline but there isn't."

While Brian examined the ground in a 15-foot radius around the outline, I scrutinised a small discoloration in the dirt just a metre off the road from the body. "The body must've been moved from where she landed. There's a small patch of blood here but not consistent with the wound."

Brian joined me, his search having turned up nothing.

I stood up, my mind racing. "This changes things for me."

"Why?" Brian asked.

"An element of doubt."

"What that it happened here?"

"Yes, or if it happened at all."

We were heading back to the car when something on the road caught my attention. Kneeling down for a closer look, I called Brian over.

"Wait, Brian ... check this out. What is it?"

"That's a wad of chewing tobacco."

"Let's mark it. Could be evidence." I jotted down the details in my notepad, noting the two pieces of evidence we had found.

Our next stop was the Black Dog music room to have a chat with Cowboy.

We parked outside, waiting for the band to arrive.

"Do you know Cowboy personally?" I asked Brian.

"Yeah, he's been around the local scene, jumping between bands. Think an Axel Rose look-a-like from the 80s but with a Cowboy hat and more tattoos. Nowhere near the same quality of voice, of course."

"What kind of music do they play?"

"Country rock, mostly. What you'd expect 'round here."

Just then, three cars pulled up, including a striking red 1963 Ford Galaxy, which Brian identified as Cowboy's. We approached him as he stepped out.

"Hey Cowboy," Brian greeted. "This is Axis Stone, a private detective from back east. He wants a word."

Cowboy sized me up with a disinterested glance. His resemblance to Axel Rose was uncanny, right down to the long brown hair under his cream, wrangler, tycoon, double cowboy hat, tasselled vest, and numerous tattoos. Noticing scratches on his forehead, I got straight to the point.

"I'm investigating the murder of Wendy Ram. I believe she was your former girlfriend."

"Yeah, so? There's been a few," he replied nonchalantly.

"Were they all murdered?" I shot back cynically.

"Ha, what are you, a comedian?" He quipped.

"Where were you on the night she was murdered?"

"Last Friday? Uh ... we had a gig at the Bluebird. You can check it out."

"And after the gig?"

"Had a few drinks with the boys."

"Can they vouch for you?"

"Ask them."

"I will. These your wheels?"

"Yeah."

"Nice," I observed.

"Would've cost a pretty penny ... Didn't you buy it from Johnny Ram?" Brian asked.

"My stepfather, yeah, so what?" he answered truculently.

"Did you use it last Friday night to get to and from the gig?" I asked.

"No. Don't take the car to gigs ... don't want to risk fans messing with it."

"How did you get those scratches on your face?"

The question caused him to look nervous; fidgety. He reached into his vest pocket, took out a rolled-up brown packet, opened it, and put some of the contents in his mouth.

"Just mucking around," he said, avoiding my gaze and chewing like a cow on cud.

"Do you own a gun?"

"Do fish swim?"

"Did you have it on you last Friday night?"

"No, it's not useful on stage," he said being smart.

With that, he walked off to join his bandmates.

Brian waved over one of the guys and shook his hand. "Axis Stone, private detective. This is Noisy Lincoln, audio engineer for the Rollers and a whole bunch of other artists 'round town."

We shook hands. I asked Noisy about last Friday night. "Did all the boys go for a drink afterwards?"

"You an Aussie?"

"Guilty as charged," said jokingly, "most folks think I'm a Brit," I admitted.

A short, skinny, full-bearded fella, with piercing blue eyes, all under a large-brimmed cowboy hat that was too big for his head. His cowboy boots were well-worn. He smiled and said, "Not me, man. I've got a bunch of Aussie muso mates; quite a few of them in Nashville, you know ... So, yeah, I mixed the Rollers at the Bluebird. I didn't go for a drink; I had to load out ... but yeah, all except Cowboy. I think he said something about catching some other act downtown ... don't recall which one."

"Cool, thanks, Noisy," I said, piecing together the night's events.

As Noisy walked off, I turned to Brian with a question that had been nagging at me. "Was Cowboy eating chewing tobacco just now?"

"Sure was," Brian confirmed. "Stokers Tennessee original, I reckon. He's always got a wad of that shit in his mouth."

This piece of information clicked something in my mind.

"Brian, the wad we found at the crime scene ... you think it could be Cowboy's?"

Brian pondered for a moment, then replied, "It's possible. He's known for that brand."

The potential connection was too strong to ignore. Cowboy's presence at the crime scene, if proven, could change the entire direction of the investigation.

"We need to get the cops to test that wad for DNA," I said, already thinking ahead to the next steps. "If we could link Cowboy to the scene—"

Brian nodded in agreement. "Yeah, and the blood patch, it's

starting to paint a different picture of what might've happened there that night."

The pieces were slowly falling into place, the scratches on Cowboy's face, his edginess, but I knew we had to tread carefully. Linking Cowboy to the crime scene was crucial, but we needed more concrete evidence to make a solid case.

"Let's get back to the Conrad; I need to call the cops," I suggested. "We need to move fast on this."

Brian started the car, and we headed back, each lost in our thoughts about the case and the new lead that had just opened up.

CHAPTER SIX

Charlie had decided to meet up with Serina Sun to discuss the case. She was on the set of 'Woman of the Night' at Pegasus Studios, located on the Paramount Studios lot. Instructed to enter through the Bronson Gate on Melrose, his name was already cleared with security at the gate.

The process went smoothly. The guard at the gate provided directions to the visitor car park and to Stage 3. Walking through the busy lot to Stage 3, Charlie was soon granted entry into the bustling environment of a live set.

Inside, the set depicted a bedroom scene—a double bed that appeared recently slept in, low lighting, and a window simulating the red neon glow of a street outside. It was convincing, resembling either a bedsit in Lower Manhattan or a cheap hotel room there. A jib crane with a digital camera mounted on it and an operator below dominated the set. Nearby, four director's chairs were occupied, likely reviewing the script for the upcoming scene. The art department busily added the finishing touches to the bedroom set, while the director of photography and his team sorted the lighting. The crew around seemed to be in a state of prepared waiting.

A young woman, bespectacled and with a clipboard clutched to her chest, approached Charlie. "Hi, are you Mr Chan?" she asked in a squeaky Bronx accent.

"Yes," Charlie replied, knowing his presence there was somewhat out of place.

"Follow me, please," she said, leading him past a hive of activity, including carpenters and grips, to a dressing room door. After a quick knock and a brief check inside, she gestured for Charlie to enter.

Inside the dressing room, Serina Sun sat in front of a large mirror, wrapped in a silver robe with her hair in a towel. A special effects makeup artist was applying a gruesomely realistic gash down the side of her face and a cut throat from ear to ear.

"That's looking nasty, Serina," Charlie commented.

"Hi Charlie, yeah, I die on set today, quite literally. Think it looks convincing?" Serina joked.

"Very believable," Charlie affirmed.

"Lucy, this is my private detective Charlie Chan. He's done some acting as well," Serina introduced.

Lucy, a small girl with brown mousey hair, dressed in a blue T-shirt and jeans, looked up from her work. "Hey Charlie," she greeted.

Charlie leaned against the vanity table, preferring to speak with Serina directly rather than through her reflection. "Have you had time to think about the case since we spoke on the phone, Serina?"

"Not really Charlie, I can only cram so much into this blonde's brain of mine, and right now it's full of my lines," she said jokingly. "What do you recommend?"

Charlie explained the situation. "It sounds like a B-grade movie plot, but if it's legit, we could get the other party to sign a document giving you a percentage of whatever is found. However, the real money might be in the screenplay this guy is writing."

Serina's interest piqued. "Then I want to read the treatment. If it's doable and the players are serious, I'll consider a supporting female lead role, with a guarantee written into the script."

Charlie mentioned the writer's secrecy but noted that his private detective, Gerri Jewel, had confirmed script development funding from a studio.

"Gerri, is that a he or a...?" Serina started to ask.

"A she," Charlie clarified.

"Well, she should be able to show confirmation of that. I'll sign an NDA if needed," Serina decided. "With 'Woman of the Night' raising my profile, they should be thrilled at the prospect of having me."

Just then, the bespectacled PA popped her head in. "On set now, Miss Sun."

Lucy, having finished the makeup, gave Serina a reassuring tap. "Go break a leg, darling."

Charlie couldn't help but think how the special effects made it look like someone had run amok with a carving knife. As Serina posed, he snapped a couple of shots with his phone.

"You look deadly," he complimented.

"Thank you, darling. Do you want to stay for the scene?" Serina offered.

"Love to," Charlie accepted, following her out. The crew from hair, wardrobe, and makeup swarmed around Serina as she made her way to the set.

She was greeted by a warm round of applause from the crew and cast members. It was a pivotal moment—the last scene of 'Woman of the Night', where her character meets a tragic end. The scene was intense, with her character being murdered by a stalker, a woman driven mad by unrequited love, someone Serina's character had never suspected.

Charlie, having been introduced to the director, was given a chair to watch the filming. The scene unfolded with gripping tension, and he couldn't help but admire Serina's skill in front of the camera.

Upon returning to the office, Charlie found Carmen and Gerri Jewel comfortably seated in the lounge area, engaged in conversation.

"Ladies," Charlie greeted, taking a seat alongside them.

"How was our Woman of the Night?" Carmen asked with a hint of humour.

"Died on stage," Charlie replied dryly.

Gerri, momentarily taken aback, thought they were discussing an actual murder. Noticing her shock, Charlie quickly explained he was referring to Serina's scene in the movie.

He then mentioned Serina's condition for moving forward with the case, which hinged on her client's willingness to provide the information she requested. Gerri, understanding the gravity of the situation, agreed to discuss it with her client and promised to get back to them with a response.

As they chatted, the dynamics in the room shifted slightly, the weight of the case and its complexities becoming more apparent. Charlie knew that how they proceeded next could make all the difference in unravelling the truth behind the mysterious case.

~ ~ ~

Brian had a few errands to run, so I used the time to settle into my room at the Conrad. I needed to speak with law enforcement, but given Detective Miller's previous disinterest, I decided to contact Sheriff Don Tanner directly. His secretary managed to secure me a meeting at his personal office on 2nd Street, just walking distance from the Conrad. This time, I dressed more appropriately to avoid the discomfort of the heat.

Soon, I found myself sitting in the reception outside the Sheriff's office. The door swung open and a tall figure in uniform, adorned with a massive grey moustache, waved me into his office. The air was tense as I sat opposite him, feeling the weight of his surly demeanour.

"I heard about you from Detective Miller, son," he started gruffly. "I believe he warned you not to poke your nose where it doesn't belong."

"Sheriff Tanner," I replied calmly, "I'm just doing my job. Your daughter hired me because she believes Ziggy Stardust is innocent of the charges against him."

"My daughter wouldn't know her ass from her elbow," he dismissed.

"I beg to differ, sir. I find her quite intelligent. I don't want to cause any trouble, but I've found new evidence that might prove her claim."

He seemed to soften slightly. "Where you from, son?"

"I was born in New York but raised in Sydney, Australia. I sort of straddle those two places."

His demeanour shifted positively. "I thought I recognised that accent. Some of my best friends are Aussies. Served with them in Nam, especially at the Battle of Long Tan. They saved my ass more than once. We have reunions every ten years; last one was in Sydney. Hell of a time, though not many of us left now," he said, a touch of sadness in his voice. "Your father serve in the forces?"

"World War II, but he passed away in the late 1980s," I informed him.

"Sorry to hear that," he said genuinely. "Okay, tell me what you've got. To be honest, I'm tired of fighting with my daughter..."

I laid out everything I had learned, from the new evidence to my suspicions about Cowboy. He listened intently, especially to the part about the scratches on Cowboy's face and my speculations about the night of the murder. Whether it was my Australian background or the compelling nature of the evidence, he seemed won over. He introduced me to his deputy and summoned a CSI team. Together, we drove to the crime scene to collect the marked evidence.

After ensuring the CSI team would process the chewing tobacco for DNA and verify the blood as Wendy's, I decided to unwind at the Thistle and Rye bar at the Conrad with a JD. My relaxation was briefly interrupted by a call from Charlie, updating me on his latest intriguing case. It seemed he had everything under control and mentioned that all was well at the new Hong Kong office.

After a cosy chat with Patricia, I was about to order another drink when Sheriff's Deputy Lois Pointer called with concerning news. She had obtained CCTV footage of Cowboy and his mates at AJ's Good Time Bar on Broadway, timestamped from 12:15 am until closing at 2:30 am on the night of the murder. This footage put a dent in the perfect alibi Cowboy had, leaving an unaccounted hour, but still not enough, the Deputy felt, to commit the murder as envisaged. The Deputy was waiting on additional CCTV footage from outside The Local to see if it captured a confrontation between Cowboy and Wendy after Eo's gig.

With these thoughts in mind, I decided to freshen up with a shower before dinner. Returning to my room, I found a note slipped under the door from Brian, asking to meet at his studio at 7 pm. Glancing at the clock, I realised I had no time for a shower and hurried to his studio on South Street, Music Row.

Finding the place in the night's darkness took nearly fifteen minutes. Brian's car wasn't there yet, so I waited outside, expecting him any minute. Suddenly, a car pulled up, and two men rushed out, attacking me with baseball bats. The beating was ferocious; I had no chance to defend myself and went down under the assault, instinctively trying to protect my face, which meant my body took the brunt of the blows. I must have blacked out because when I regained consciousness, I was lying on the ground in agony. Attempting to stand revealed the excruciating pain in my ribs ... I called Deputy Pointer.

She arrived quickly, helping me into her patrol car and taking me to the hospital. An X-ray confirmed that, fortunately, my ribs were bruised, not broken.

Back at the hotel, a look in the bathroom mirror showed the extent of the damage to my face. I struggled to undress, my hands painfully sore from taking the brunt of the hits. I made my way into the shower, sitting on the floor under the warm water, hoping it would alleviate some of the pain. It didn't.

Waking up the next morning was an ordeal. Every movement sent waves of pain through my battered body. Somehow, I managed to drag myself to the bathroom. The mirror reflected the extent of last night's brutality—my face and body were a canvas of black and blue.

As I was assessing the damage, the house phone rang, jarring me from my thoughts. It was Deputy Pointer on the other end. "Lois, I feel like I've been through a mincer," I grimaced into the receiver. "Okay, I'll meet you downstairs in an hour."

Dressing was a slow, laborious process, but I eventually made it down to the Blue Aster. A quick breakfast accompanied by what felt like three hundred coffees barely brought me back to life.

An hour later, true to her word, Deputy Pointer was waiting for me outside the hotel. Wearing dark sunglasses to disguise my black eyes, I walked out to meet her, each step measured and cautious, trying to hide the extent of my pain.

CHAPTER
SEVEN

The NDA from Jewel Investigations had arrived via email. Carmen printed it out and handed a copy each to Charlie and Enzo. They congregated around the lounge area, each studying the document with a critical eye.

"Seems fine to me," Charlie finally said, breaking the silence.

"But why are we the ones signing this, not Serina?" Enzo questioned, looking up from the pages.

Carmen, ever the voice of reason, reminded them, "Because we have a contract with Serina. It's standard procedure in cases like this."

After they had sent back the signed NDA, another email arrived from Gerri Jewel, this time including a twelve-page story treatment by Kane Stevenson. Carmen, with her usual efficiency, immediately searched for Stevenson on IMDBPro and was impressed by his credentials.

She printed out the treatment and distributed copies to Charlie and Enzo. "The writer, Kane Stevenson, has an Oscar nomination and an Emmy under his belt. He's not just a rank amateur."

Once they had all read through the treatment, Charlie was the first to share his thoughts. "I see why the map is essential; without it, the story lacks substance."

"But where does Serina fit into all this?" Enzo wondered aloud.

"I was thinking the same," Carmen agreed. "The story doesn't seem to have a place for her. He could just fictionalise the map's discovery."

"What if the whole thing is a ploy?" Charlie suddenly proposed. "Remember the failed attempt from Hong Kong to search for the treasure under the pretence of a film shoot? This could be a more credible attempt."

"You're right, much of the story revolves around Zhang Yan," Enzo pointed out.

"And there's no prominent role for Serina, except maybe Luo Yan," Carmen noted.

"She asked to be written into the script," Charlie recalled. "With Stevenson's writing skills, I'm sure he could create a role for her."

"That makes sense," Enzo conceded.

Charlie stood up and went to the side table, pouring three glasses of red wine. He handed them out, raising his glass, "Well, let's drink to a successful resolution of this peculiar case."

Carmen jumped up, her business sense kicking in. "I'll send the treatment to Serina first," she said, heading to her desk to forward the email.

The three of them toasted, the air filled with a mix of anticipation and uncertainty about where this unusual case would lead them next.

The following morning, Charlie was reading the LA Times while having breakfast. Carmen wandered out in a robe and bare feet, looking as though she'd had a rough night. He lowered the paper, his concern evident. "You okay?"

"No, I don't feel well this morning, hon," she replied, her voice reflecting her discomfort.

"Why don't you stay at home? Come in later if you feel up to it," Charlie suggested kindly.

She gave him a peck on the cheek and then sat in a wicker chair, staring at the sun glinting off the blue water of the swimming pool. Charlie leaned forward in his chair as though he'd spotted a photo of himself in the paper. "What's this?"

He handed the paper to Carmen. Her eyes widened as she read. "What!" she exclaimed in disbelief. "That didn't take her long. And listen to this, 'Serina hasn't yet accepted the lead role, but is confident contracts will soon be signed. I Captain Kidd you not! joked Serina Sun' ... can you believe that? The article must have come from publicity at Pegasus, Selina isn't that stupid, is she?"

Charlie's expression turned serious. "What worries me is if Luo Yan and her sons in LA didn't know about the map before, they certainly would now. Do you recall Zhong's warning?"

Carmen nodded solemnly, fully grasping the severity of the situation. The newspaper article had catapulted their case into the spotlight, potentially alerting individuals with conceivably dangerous intentions.

~ ~ ~

"I advise you to go home, Mr Stone. You've obviously stepped on some toes here, and I have no desire to be investigating your murder next," Sheriff Tanner told me in no uncertain terms. I was in his office with Deputy Pointer, receiving the dressing-down.

"I'm sorry, Sheriff, but I'm from the old school; the beating tells me I'm onto something. I've been in worse situations; I can handle it. But your advice is, of course, taken on board."

"Have it your way, but as you've experienced, there are limitations to our protection. What are your thoughts, Deputy?"

"Well, sir, whoever did this set Mr Stone up. The note under the door, the location. If they were out to kill him, they would've. It was a warning to stop whatever he's doing, and that had to be pursuing Travis Norton."

The Sheriff rubbed his face, thinking. "Is he known to have associations?"

"His stepfather is Johnny Ram, the younger brother of Cyrus Ram."

"Yeah, well, we know all about him, don't we? Go pay him a visit, at least it'll be letting him know we've made the connection."

"Yes sir," Pointer said.

"Where are we up to with Norton?"

"There's a suspicious one-hour window of opportunity for him to have perpetrated the crime, sir. I asked for CCTV from out front of The Local to confirm he met with the deceased, but it's gone missing."

"Is it private or council?" the Sheriff asked.

"Council, sir," Pointer answered.

"Obviously, there's a conspiracy here to protect Norton, but without strong evidence, I can't drop the charges on Stardust. You'll need to get me something more solid, Deputy."

I sat in silence, thinking, while Deputy Pointer drove us through town. "What's your spin on this, Pointer?"

"To be honest, you're up against it. One of the richest and most influential men in Tennessee wants retribution for the murder of his daughter."

"That's what doesn't make sense. If Cowboy's the perp, why are the Rams protecting him?"

"Can only be he didn't do it."

"No, that doesn't wash with me. No, there's more to it than meets the eye. What if it wasn't Cowboy? What if it was someone sent to frighten Wendy and it went wrong, or someone sent to frame Eo?"

"You'll get yourself killed thinking like that, Stone."

I glanced at her, for the first time seeing past the uniform at the woman. She wasn't tall, mid-thirties, single—I guessed—attractive, with black hair in a pixie cut, exuding confidence and courage. Could be gay, I thought.

"You married, Pointer?"

"Getting personal, are we?"

"Just asking."

She pulled the car into Ram Motors, a second-hand dealership. Parking the car, but before getting out, she confided, "No, and yes, I'm gay."

What perception, I thought, then struggled out of the car.

"You keep quiet, I'll do the talking," she directed.

We walked through the lot and entered the office. The uniform meant we weren't given any attention. Pointer approached a salesman seated behind his desk.

"Hey, Reno, boss in?"

"Yeah, Lois, he's out back in the workshop. Just go through."

I followed her through the building into the workshop. There were cars up on hoists, workers detailing cars, and a thickset guy in a suit standing beside a red 1973 Corvette Stingray with its hood up, looking at the engine.

Pointer approached him. "Johnny, nice wheels. She yours?"

Without looking away from the car, he said in a gruff voice, "Someone is asking a lot of money for her on a trade for that," pointing his thumb over his shoulder at a British racing green Aston Martin DB6 up on the hoist.

"That a 1966?" I asked.

"No, '65, Grand Tourer," he growled.

He turned from the car and faced us. The left cheek of his thin face was scarred, his eyes were like a shark's. This guy, dressed in a dapper grey suit, white T, had criminal written all over him.

"This an official visit?" he snarled.

"Just a few questions..." Pointer said calmly.

He walked off towards a small office. A quick, aggressive gesture from him sent the office girl and a worker in overalls out in a hurry. He sat down behind the messy desk and glared up at us.

"Right. So?"

"This is Mr Axis Stone, a private detective from back east here investigating Wendy's murder."

"Isn't that done and dusted?"

"There's new evidence."

"That won't impress my brother; he's been waiting for that Stardust bum to swing."

"Mr Stone was beat up last night; thought you might have heard something?"

"I think Mr Stone should go home, or it won't be just a beating," he said, drilling me with his eyes.

I returned serve. "That sounds like a threat, Mr Ram."

That fired him up. "Call it what you like, Stone. We don't need some New York gumshoe sticking his nose in our business. You got it? That'll be all, Pointer. Next time, make a fucking appointment."

He got up and bumped past me as he left.

On the way back to the car park, I remarked, "You said I was from back east, he said New York..." I left that fact hanging for Deputy Pointer to absorb.

In the car on our way back to town, I got a call from Brian. He'd heard about the beating and was concerned, especially since it occurred outside his studio, making him feel responsible.

I asked Pointer, "Where can we meet Brian for a coffee?"

"Tell him the Bobby, we'll be there in five minutes. He'll know it."

We found Brian holding a us table in the alfresco section of the Bobby Café. We sat down and ordered coffees.

"Hey, Brian," Pointer greeted.

"Looking good, Lois. Heard you rescued our Mr Stone here. You alright, you're looking awful, Axis?"

"Thanks but I'll live."

"What were you doing at the studio in the first place?" Brian asked.

"I got this..." I handed him the note I'd received.

"Who would be using me to set you up?"

"Has to be someone connected to Cowboy," I replied, just as the coffees were delivered.

While sugaring her coffee, Pointer said, "We just paid Johnny Ram a visit."

"Now there's a likely suspect," Brian commented warily. "You know if folks who buy a car from him miss payments they get a beating from him or his cronies?"

"All too familiar ... Collusion creates confusion, even the car park CCTV from The Local has conveniently gone missing," I groaned.

Brian asked Pointer, "Who said that, Tony?"

"Yes."

"Twenty bucks would buy him," Brian said with disdain. "What were you hoping it would show?"

"Cowboy having a row with Wendy," Pointer asserted.

"I saw that," Brian admitted.

That sparked interest from us. I leaned forward in my chair. "You did?"

"I was loading out my gear into the Kombi and heard them. They were in Beano's car arguing."

"Beano?"

"The Rollers' drummer," Brian explained.

"Alone?"

"Yes, by the time I went back inside and then out again with the next load, say five minutes max, Cowboy was gone."

"Where was Wendy?" Pointer inquired.

"She was sitting alone in Eo's car, well, Sherri's car."

I said firmly to Pointer, "We have our witness." Pointer immediately stood up, pulled out her phone, and walked out of earshot of Brian and myself, dialling the Sheriff, I presumed.

She returned to her seat moments later and announced, "The DNA on the tobacco and blood will be in tomorrow. I need to swab Norton."

"After the attack on you, Axis, and Johnny Ram's reaction, that'll definitely stir things up," Brian said gravely.

"I wonder if it was Beano's car used in the abduction?" I pondered.

"We could check the tyre tracks at the crime scene," Pointer proposed.

I suggested, "The car should be checked for traces of Wendy's blood anyway."

Pointer asked Brian, "Beano is Cowboy's cousin, isn't he?"

"Yep, so is the bass player in the band, Raddo. He and Beano are brothers; they live together … from memory Cowboy camps there as well."

~ ~ ~

Sitting back in his office chair with a perplexed look, Charlie hung up the phone. "I can't believe that."

From behind her desk, Carmen inquired, "Why, what did Serina say?"

"She said it was her new agent. He decided a little press would do her good."

"Responsible is the word missing," Carmen remarked.

Carol sauntered into the office, dressed in a vivid orange, blue, and black stretchy African Ankara Dashiki Kente print dress, her hair worn up.

"Wow, Carol, I need sunglasses to look at that dress," Charlie joked.

Carol chuckled and struck a playful modelling pose for him and Carmen. "Miss Jewel has asked for a meeting with you and Serina at Serina's house at 4 this afternoon."

"This'll be the official search. I'll text Serina and see if she can make it. I was just speaking to her; she's at Pegasus, it's the 'Woman of the Night' wrap party," Charlie said, texting.

"That sounds like fun," Carol remarked, always keen to party.

By the time Carol had returned to reception, Charlie had received a response and called out to her, "Let Miss Jewel know that'll be fine. Then get Enzo to meet us there."

CHAPTER
EIGHT

Pointer and I met with Crime Scene Investigation Lieutenant Ted Way at the Police Forensic Services Division, on Gass Boulevard.

"We didn't take tyre impressions of the crime scene because, at the time, it was deemed unnecessary," Way stated dismissively.

"Was it 3D mapped?" I asked.

"Yes, but that won't show tyre marks. We'll need to send out a team. Is the Sheriff aware of this? We already sent out a team for the other evidence; the tobacco and blood."

"I also need the vehicle owned by Beano Curtis processed with luminol for blood traces, and a DNA swab from Travis Norton," Pointer detailed.

Lieutenant Way didn't seem thrilled with the additional workload.

On the way back to the car, Pointer said, "I keep waiting for a call from the Sheriff; you'd have to expect Cyrus Ram to have been in his ear by now."

"How would he react to that?"

"Not sure, Cyrus Ram has influence with the governor and the mayor, and they have influence with the Sheriff. Add to that, because of his daughter, Sheriff Tanner doesn't think too highly of your Ziggy Stardust."

"Hmm, speaking of Eo, any chance you can make a call to check on him?" I asked.

"Why?"

"He told me he wouldn't last long in captivity."

Pointer called from the car to check on Eo, confirming he was fine. She then planned to get a statement from Brian, proposing to drop me off at the Conrad, pick up Brian, and take him to her office. I was content with this arrangement, needing to catch up with my office, and being aware of the time difference with New York.

However, Brian requested to give his statement at the studio instead. Pointer agreed, and I chose to accompany her since it was on the way to the Conrad.

We arrived at the studio and parked beside Brian's Kombi. Noticing a white van parked a few spaces away in the loading bay to the studio, we approached the entrance. Just as I was about to open the side door, gunshots rang out from inside. Pointer instantly switched into defence mode, drawing her pistol and pushing me aside. She positioned herself by the door, gun at the ready.

Realising I was unarmed, Pointer instructed me to fetch a weapon from the glove compartment in her car. I limped to the car, retrieved the pistol, and was heading back when someone burst out of the studio door.

As Pointer ordered the figure to stop, she was suddenly shot twice. The impact of the bullets propelled her backwards against the van, causing her to hit the side panel hard before sliding down onto the ground. I quickly took cover around the corner of the building, stealing a quick glance at the scene. The shooter was standing over Pointer. Seizing the moment, I stepped out and fired three bullets into him, and he collapsed.

Unexpectedly, another assailant emerged from the doorway and fired a shot at me, the bullet grazing my left bicep. I retreated back to cover. Despite my injury, I risked another look; two assailants were now helping the one I'd shot, while another opened the van door to assist the wounded man inside. I stepped into the alleyway and emptied the remainder of my clip at them. Most bullets hit the van, but one struck an assailant in the shoulder. He managed to get into the van, which then quickly reversed and sped away. My clip was empty; all I could do was watch it disappear.

Limping with difficulty, I approached Pointer, finding her barely conscious. She had been shot in the gut, and the situation was dire. Blood seeped from her mouth, indicating massive internal haemorrhaging. Fighting to stay awake, she tried to speak, and I read her lips mouthing the name 'Johnny Ram'. She pointed a shaking finger at the gun in my hand. I sat on the ground, cradling her head and holding her bloodied hand. Then, I placed my gun in her hand. She gripped it firmly. I also put her other gun back in her holster. Now, I couldn't be charged. Tears welled in my eyes as I watched the life fade from her eyes; Deputy Lois Pointer died in my arms. Overwhelmed with grief, I barely felt my own physical pain.

With immense effort, I rose and limped into the studio to check on Brian. The sight was heart-wrenching; Brian sat dead at his console, shot in the forehead and chest. The chaos and tragedy of the scene were overwhelming. Pointer and Brian were dead, and I was injured. But in that moment of profound sorrow, I vowed through gritted teeth to avenge Lois and Brian's deaths. What a senseless waste it all was.

~ ~ ~

Charlie and Carmen arrived at Serina's house promptly at 4 pm. They sat in the car on the driveway, awaiting the arrival of the others. The familiar sound of Enzo's black, custom Softail Harley Davidson soon broke the silence as he parked behind them. As Enzo dismounted his bike, a Mercedes SUV pulled into the driveway, with Serina stepping out accompanied by her new agent. Shortly after, a taxi arrived, dropping off Gerri Jewel and a middle-aged man.

Gathered at the doorstep, introductions were made. Serina introduced her new agent, Lucian Grange, while Charlie introduced his team along with Gerri Jewel, who in turn introduced screenwriter Kane Stevenson.

Serina unlocked the front door, only for the group to be

confronted with a shocking scene — the interior of the house had been completely ransacked. They entered, taken aback by the sheer extent of the devastation. Furniture was upturned, carpets ripped up, and even some floorboards were pried open. Overwhelmed, Serina burst into tears and was escorted outside by her agent.

"Guess we've been beaten to the punch," Kane remarked despondently.

Enzo nodded in agreement. "Definitely, but this wasn't the work of a single individual. It would've taken a whole crew of treasure hunters."

"Indeed, it must have been done while Serina was at the wrap party," Charlie deduced. "They were thorough, even took out the security cameras."

"The price of publicity," Carmen reflected sombrely.

"How true," Gerri agreed.

Kane, looking thoughtful, asked, "I wonder if they found the map?"

Charlie responded, "Well, if they did, we'll probably never know. However, if they didn't..."

"Then we'd have an enemy," Enzo concluded, finishing Charlie's thought.

Charlie gave Gerri and Kane a lift back to the Sunset office, while Lucian took Serina back to the wrap party. Charlie wanted to give Lucian a piece of his mind over the publicity release that caused the problem but decided it wasn't the appropriate time.

At the office, Kane initiated the discussion. "Who do you think was responsible, Charlie?" he asked.

Kane, a good-looking man with a friendly demeanour, epitomised a writer. His keen attention to detail and attentive listening skills were a testament to his profession. Charlie found him likable.

"I think it was the work of the Zhang Yan family. From your research, you must know his widow, Luo Yan, lives in LA with her two sons," Charlie replied.

"Yes, but I haven't reached out to her yet," Kane admitted.

"I need to ask you, Kane, and please be honest, are you writing a legitimate film script, or is it a cover for a treasure hunt?" Charlie inquired.

Kane and Gerri exchanged a glance.

"Before you answer him, consider the risks we're taking, potentially up against serious criminals," Carmen interjected.

"Okay, look," Kane leaned forward in his seat, "it's both. The bonus would be finding Kidd's treasure, but the project isn't dependent on finding it."

"Right, thank you for your honesty. How would you write Serina into your screenplay, considering the treatment reads with a Hong Kong bias?" Charlie asked.

"I plan for the main plot to mirror what we're all doing, fictionalised, of course, with your approval. Serina would play Gerri's role, as a female private investigator," Kane explained.

Carmen rolled her eyes.

"That makes sense," Enzo commented. "But will the budget stretch to afford Vin Diesel to play me?" The group burst into laughter.

After the laughter died down, Gerri asked, "Charlie, do you think we should reach out to Luo Yan?"

"We have a Hong Kong office manned by a former senior detective of the Hong Kong Organised Crime and Triad Bureau, the OTCB. Zhong is probably the most informed person on Hong Kong crime families on the planet. It would be prudent to first seek his advice," Charlie suggested.

Gerri and Kane nodded, agreeing to reconvene at Charlie's discretion.

Once Gerri and Kane had departed, Charlie checked the time. It was 6 pm Thursday in LA and 10 am Friday in Hong Kong. Deciding it was a good time to call, he phoned the Cat Street office, where PA Laila Sing answered.

"Hello from Hollywood, Laila, how are you?" Charlie greeted, putting her on speaker for Carmen and Enzo to hear.

Laila's voice came through the speaker. "It's been very quiet here until one of Zhong's friends at Hong Kong Police handed us a case … Oh, and I commence my master of social sciences in criminology at the University of Hong Kong next week."

"Good for you, Laila. Can you put me through to Zhong?" Charlie asked.

"Hello, Charlie," Zhong greeted as he came on the line.

"Laila said you've got your first case?" Charlie inquired.

"Yes, the 18-year-old daughter of a prominent local family has been missing for three months, and the police haven't found any trace of her."

"What are you thinking?" Charlie asked.

"She's probably shacked up with a boyfriend on Lantau Island."

"You could put your money on it," Charlie chuckled. "Listen, Zhong, do you remember the Captain Kidd's treasure map case?"

"Yes."

"Well, the house where it's alleged Knight hid the maps was just ransacked, we suspect by thugs connected to Zhang Yan."

"Luo Yan, I did warn you about her," Zhong reminded.

"Our client, the actress Serina Sun, has a new agent who leaked the story of the hidden map to the press."

"An open invitation for crackpots and for Luo Yan," Zhong noted.

"My question is, how should we deal with Luo Yan? Should we confront her?"

"Yes, do a deal now before it gets ugly. But make sure it's complete — all signed, sealed, and delivered. Because if you don't, she's more than capable of unleashing hell."

Enzo chimed in. "Hey, Zhong, it's Enzo here. What if she won't play ball?"

"Then you'll have a war on your hands, Enzo, if you haven't already. That's assuming she doesn't already have the map."

"That's the conundrum; we've got no way of knowing that."

"You need to proceed assuming it hasn't been found. That way, you'll quickly get your answer about whether she's got it," Zhong advised.

Charlie nodded in agreement with Zhong's logic. "Thanks, Zhong. Good luck with your case."

~ ~ ~

"Look at you, Stone. Beat up, shot ... we've lost one of our finest, and then Brian X," Sheriff Tanner remarked emotionally from behind his desk.

"Doesn't that tell you something, Sheriff? We touched a nerve. I know who did this," I insisted.

"No, Stone, there'll be no vigilante actions in my town, if that's what you're thinking."

My frustration was palpable, and I couldn't hold back. "He murdered our witness, murdered your deputy ... deputise me, let me finish this."

Sheriff Tanner seemed to recognise my passion and appeared to appreciate it. "Look, so far I've tolerated your involvement. Private detectives in Tennessee must be licensed by the Tennessee Private Investigation and Polygraph Commission, and you're not."

"Sir, you know my intentions are righteous," I appealed.

I could tell by his expression that he was seriously considering my appeal.

"I have the authority to appoint special deputies under Tennessee Code Annotated, Title 8, Chapter 8, Part 10. It's up to my discretion to determine who is qualified to serve as a special deputy. It's ultimately my decision if a private detective can be appointed as a special deputy on a short-term basis. That person must adhere to the rules and regulations set forth by the sheriff's office and the state of Tennessee."

"I will, sir."

"Okay." He opened a drawer, took out a badge, and handed it to me. "You'll be issued a registered firearm by the command staff."

"Thank you, Sheriff. One more thing, will you consider releasing Eo under the provision that he leaves Nashville and releases the girls in his commune? The only thing he's guilty of is helping teenagers to find themselves."

"I'll take that on advisedness. And one other stipulation from me, Special Deputy Stone: you will agree to select a partner from the six detectives here."

I pondered the offer for a moment. "My choice?"

"Yes, your choice."

CHAPTER NINE

The six detectives, four men and two women, all younger than thirty and dressed in full uniform, stood in line before me, radiating pride and readiness. Among them, one in particular captured my attention, as if mentally signalling me. I asked for her name.

"Rita Suarez, sir," she responded with crisp, military precision.

"Meet me at the Blue Aster, Conrad Hotel, 7 tomorrow morning for breakfast. Dress in civvies," I instructed.

Rita nodded in acknowledgment, her expression remaining professional and focused.

Turning back to the sheriff's staff, I inquired about the next step. "Now, who's going to issue me a weapon?"

~ ~ ~

With her home in disarray, Serina was staying at the Mondrian Hotel in West Hollywood. Meanwhile, Charlie took the opportunity to have Enzo search her house for the map while he himself attempted to contact Luo Yan.

It was an arduous morning before Carol finally located a contact number. Upon calling, a maid answered. Charlie requested Luo Yan and was put on hold. A man's voice eventually responded. Charlie introduced himself and inquired about the man's identity, receiving only a curt, 'what do you want?' in reply. Assuming the man was representing Luo Yan, Charlie proposed a meeting. They agreed to meet for lunch at Merois in West Hollywood, a restaurant familiar to Charlie on Sunset Boulevard, quite near the office. The man finally introduced himself as Niko Yan.

Enzo approached the front door of Serina's house, key in hand. As he inserted it into the lock, the door nudged open, revealing it was unlocked. He quickly surveyed the street, noting a black Mitsubishi Outlander SUV with tinted windows, unable to determine if it was occupied. Pistol drawn, Enzo cautiously entered the house, pausing in the foyer to assess the situation. The disarray remained unchanged. Listening intently, he heard a creak from the second-storey floorboards.

Navigating the mess, he ascended the staircase with the stealth of a SWAT officer, careful not to alert any potential intruder. Each step was deliberate and silent, as the slightest noise could betray his presence. The tension in the air was palpable, and his grip on his weapon tightened, ready to react at a moment's notice.

The house was unnervingly quiet, with only the subtle creaking of the old floorboards under his feet breaking the silence. His eyes darted around, scanning the shadows cast by the dim light, alert to any movement. He controlled his breathing, trying to calm the adrenaline rush that sharpened his focus yet threatened to overwhelm him.

As Enzo reached the top of the staircase, he paused, his ears straining for any sound that might indicate the presence of the intruder. The stillness was almost suffocating, creating a sense of impending confrontation. He was acutely aware that around the next corner, a potentially armed and dangerous individual might be waiting.

In this heightened state of alertness, Enzo prepared himself mentally and physically for what was to come. The uncertainty of the situation only added to the intensity, as he braced himself for a potential life-or-death encounter.

The noise clearly emanated from the main bedroom. Gun poised,

Enzo nudged the door open and stepped inside. A man, partially hidden under the bed, cried out in alarm, pleading not to be shot.

"Come out, keeping your hands where I can see them," Enzo commanded.

The man emerged and rose to his feet, hands raised. Enzo immediately recognised him. "You're Serina's agent. What the fuck are you doing here?"

"Sorry, I should've called first. Serina asked me to look for the map," the agent, Lucian Grange, replied nervously.

Enzo's disdain was palpable. "Haven't you caused enough problems, um..."

"Grange, Lucian Grange ... Problems, what do you mean?" Grange's hands remained raised.

"You leaked the story to the press that caused this fucking mess," Enzo accused.

"It wasn't me; it was Pegasus. They're relentless about publicity."

Enzo lowered his gun. "Put your hands down. Is that your black Outlander outside?"

"Yes."

"Anyone in it?"

"No."

Enzo was relieved, he thought it might have belonged to Luo Yan. "Find anything?"

"Nothing yet. Serina asked me to check under the beds, but the carpets are all new. It doesn't make sense to find something from sixty years ago here. Are you also here to search?"

"Yes, but be careful. The Chinese family originally owning the map, whom we suspect ransacked this place, are not to be trifled with. You're in danger being here."

Grange appeared startled. "I hadn't considered that."

"You better get used to getting a bum steer working for Serina," Enzo remarked with a chuckle, his opinion of Grange softening.

"Should I leave then?" Grange inquired.

"No, stay while I'm here. Let's search logically, starting with the original décor," Enzo suggested.

Grange appreciated Enzo's approach, sensing a newfound respect for the detective's logic.

Charlie stepped into Merois restaurant atop the Pendry, an eleven-storey boutique hotel in West Hollywood. He admired the elegant décor as he waited to be seated by the maître d'. The restaurant was bustling at full capacity. The suave maître d' approached and escorted him to a table by the window, offering Charlie a stunning view of LA through the tall, floor-to-ceiling glass windows.

Shortly after being seated, a slender Chinese man in his forties, dressed in a tailored grey suit, white shirt, and black necktie, sporting a short, modern haircut and wrap-around sunglasses, joined him. Charlie immediately sensed an air of authority and danger about him, reminiscent of other triad members he had encountered. The man removed his sunglasses, revealing intense, scrutinising eyes.

"Mr Yan?" Charlie began.

"You're a private detective. What do you want with my mother, Chan?" The man's Californian accent was flawless, indicating a local upbringing.

"I represent the actress Serina Sun. Are you familiar with her?"

"Yes, so?"

"I think you know, Mr Yan. Let's cut to the chase—"

Their conversation was momentarily interrupted by the waiter to take their order. Once the waiter left, before Charlie could resume, Yan spoke up. "You own the major share in Utopia 8."

"It seems you know more about me than I do about you. Perhaps you could even the scales?"

"I am the youngest son of Zhang Yan and Luo Yan. I don't think I need to say more than that. Oh, and we didn't find the map."

"Thank you for your candour. I'm here to negotiate a deal."

Yan's gaze turned icy. "Do you have the map?"

"No, but if we agree on a deal, the owner will allow a comprehensive search."

"The map's value is uncertain. No-one knows if it's legitimate."

"It was considered legitimate enough by the Royal Hong Kong Yacht Club members to mount an expedition years ago."

"That may be, but it doesn't necessarily add value ... Your client has a producer ready to make a film, and that is valuable."

"I can't speak for the producer, but that is correct. I believe they would be interested in incorporating your family's history into the story."

Yan's eyes narrowed. "What are you proposing?"

"A syndicate, with shared ownership."

"Of the map?"

"Yes. Any treasure hunt or movie venture related to it would require the syndicate's consent."

"And the share percentages?"

"That's for negotiation. Today, we just need to agree so I can draft the heads of agreement."

As their food arrived, Yan contemplated for a moment and then said, "Okay, you have the family's approval to proceed with the agreement."

~ ~ ~

I observed Detective Rita Suarez as she approached my table, punctual as expected. It struck me how different police officers can look when out of uniform. Her civilian attire revealed a more defined figure than her uniform had suggested. She took a seat across from me.

"Good morning, sir."

"It's Axis, Rita. And good morning to you too. What would you like for breakfast? I hear the buffet is quite good," I offered.

"Just coffee, sir. I'm not one for breakfast."

I caught the waiter's attention. "I'm the same, though back in Australia, I'd have Vegemite on toast with my coffee."

"I know someone from Sydney, a singer. She always keeps a stash of Vegemite, might part with some."

"Wouldn't want to deprive her of a taste of home." The waiter brought her coffee and refilled mine.

"Have you been briefed on what we're doing?"

"Yes, sir, but only the basics."

"My goal is to apprehend Johnny Ram for the murders of Deputy Pointer and Brian X."

"Lois was a friend of mine," she disclosed.

"Then you have even more of a reason to see justice served."

"How are you so sure it was Johnny Ram?"

"His name was the last thing Lois said."

I noticed her eyes welling up with tears.

"Were you with her ... when she passed?" she asked, her voice slightly muffled behind her coffee cup.

"She died in my arms, Rita."

We shared a moment of silence, each lost in thoughts of Lois. Rita then set down her cup, her gaze fixed firmly on mine. "How do you want to play this?"

I held her gaze, considering my words carefully. "I was thinking of approaching Cyrus Ram first, giving him the opportunity to have his brother surrender peacefully."

"That would be wise," she agreed. "Directly going after Johnny would be like walking into the OK Corral. But, shouldn't the Sheriff be the one to first speak to Cyrus?" Rita questioned, considering the protocol.

"Under normal circumstances, yes, that would be the standard approach. However, given Cyrus' significant political influence, I think we might need to handle this differently," I explained.

"I understand your point," Rita acknowledged. "I actually have his number."

"Good. Let's arrange an appointment then. It's crucial we manage this carefully to avoid any unnecessary escalation or interference," I said, recognising the delicacy of the situation.

Rita nodded, understanding the gravity of our next move. "I'll make the call as soon as we finish here."

~ ~ ~

The main neon sign outside the garish, two-storey building proclaimed 'Ritzy's Hustler Club.' A smaller neon sign below announced '18+ Fully Nude.' Although officially closed during the day, the club's nocturnal activities were notorious.

Inside, on the mezzanine floor, lay the main office. This lavish space boasted two large windows at each end of the square room, offering views of the floors below. Through one window, the hustler club was visible, where, at night, young women performed pole dances on a catwalk winding between thirty tables, with additional seating flanking the catwalk. The other window overlooked a smaller, but more frequented room—an illegal gambling casino, complete with two blackjack tables, two roulette tables, a row of slot machines, a craps table, and two tables for stud poker.

The office, soundproofed and opulent, contained a large antique mahogany desk and a sunken lounge area. In the centre of the lounge area stood a fit, well-dressed man in his fifties, his black and silver hair slicked back, exuding a Hugh Hefner-like aura. Facing him, in jeans and a black jacket, was Johnny Ram, receiving a severe reprimand from his older brother, Cyrus, who was visibly irate. Another man lounged in a chair, drink in hand, observing the brothers' heated exchange.

"Are you out of your fucking mind, Johnny?" Cyrus growled.

"You told me to shut it down; I did," Johnny retorted sharply.

"No-one said anything about killing anyone, especially a police officer. Now, what are we going to do?"

Johnny shrugged nonchalantly. "Who fucking cares?"

"I'll tell you who cares." Cyrus's hand struck Johnny's face with a sharp slap. "You idiot. If the press gets wind of this, my chances of becoming governor will be obliterated," he snarled, before collapsing into a chair, leaving Johnny standing, hand on his stinging cheek, his dignity bruised in front of an audience.

Cyrus, retrieving a glass of Jack Daniel's from the coffee table, drained it in one gulp. He then turned to the man sitting opposite him and asked, "What am I going to do with this guy, Sheriff?"

~ ~ ~

"What about the DNA and tyre track results from CSI?" I inquired as we headed towards Rita's car, my pace slower than usual due to my injuries.

She dialled Lieutenant Ted Way. "Oh, and ask him about the swab from Cowboy and the blood analysis of Beano's car," I added.

She nodded. Reaching the car in the underground car park, she ended the call. "There was an issue with the DNA on the chewing tobacco."

I looked at her, one eyebrow arched in suspicion. "Don't tell me."

"You guessed it. It seems it went missing. The blood sample turned out to be from an animal."

Leaning against her car, I caught my breath after the effort of walking. "Damn, that's unfortunate on two counts … I assume that means they didn't do the swab … What about Beano's car?"

"They're working on it."

As we settled into the car, I said, "Alright, let's arrange that meeting with Cyrus … Oh, by the way, what did the newspaper report about Wendy Ram's murder?"

"Nothing," Rita responded, starting the car. "It's been kept under wraps, likely due to the governor's election in three months."

My mind was churning, trying to piece everything together.

CHAPTER
TEN

The cover-up gnawed at me incessantly, hinting at the Sheriff's complicity and casting a shadow of doubt over Rita's loyalty. Seated in Rita's car in the Conrad's dimly lit underground parking, I mulled over these unsettling thoughts as she stepped out to arrange a meeting with Cyrus Ram by phone.

The pieces of this intricate puzzle refused to align. Why would anyone orchestrate a cover-up of their own daughter's murder? Cyrus Ram's apparent apathy in pursuing her killer was baffling. The roles of Johnny Ram and Cowboy in this intricate web of deceit and violence were equally mystifying. While Lois's demise could be chalked up to a tragic mishap—a case of being in the wrong place at the wrong time— Brian's assassination was premeditated, ruthlessly executed. Perhaps he was eliminated because he witnessed the altercation between Cowboy and Wendy outside The Local on the night of the murder. And then there was the attempt on my life, likely a desperate bid to silence me as I edged closer to the truth.

My mind raced with speculations. Was Cyrus Ram masterminding this elaborate façade to safeguard his gubernatorial aspirations? Could the Sheriff be his accomplice in this charade? It struck me that the Sheriff might have his own motives for removing Eo, thereby recovering his estranged daughter. Another theory surfaced: was Cyrus plotting to exploit his daughter's murder for political sympathy, unveiling the tragedy only after pinning the crime on Eo, the presumed culprit?

Confiding my suspicions to Rita felt fraught with risk. Had she been assigned to shadow me by the Sheriff? The tampering of evidence crucial to Eo's exoneration only intensified my reluctance to trust her. For now, I was compelled to nurse these doubts in silence, proceeding with guarded caution.

Rita slid back into the car, a look of accomplishment on her face. "How did it go?"

"He was initially resistant, claiming a hectic schedule. I insisted, mentioning your critical information regarding his daughter's murder ... he conceded. We're to meet him immediately at his city office."

We pulled up at Ram Prestige, a lavish dealership displaying an array of elite vehicles from Cadillacs to Ferraris. A conspicuous Mercedes bus, emblazoned with 'Ram for Governor' in bold red lettering against a purple backdrop, dominated the front.

As we parked, a sleek-suited salesman approached, leaning in through the driver's window with an update. Mr Ram was bound for Memphis but could spare a brief window aboard his private jet at the airport. Rita glanced my way for confirmation, and I gave a subtle nod. We headed for the airport.

At Ram Aviation's hangar, we were ushered into a sumptuously appointed Cessna Citation CJ4 Gen 2 by Dianne Fisher, Ram's efficient PA. Inside the aircraft, configured for a select few, the pilot was preoccupied in the cockpit.

We settled into our seats just as Cyrus Ram, a figure exuding an aura akin to Donald Trump sans the ostentatious grin, joined us. Clad in an immaculate grey Armani suit, he offered no handshake, instead fixing me with a scrutinising stare, his face etched with the remnants of adolescent acne.

"You've got five minutes. What's this about, Suarez?"

"Sir, Detective Stone has unearthed evidence potentially absolving Ziggy Stardust."

"And what might that be, Stone? Looks to me like you came last in a buckjump at the rodeo."

Removing my sunglasses, I locked eyes with him, my bruised visage unflinching. "Here's my theory; Travis Norton was seen arguing with your daughter outside The Local at 11 pm. Following this, Sherri Tanner drove Wendy, Chaka Zuma, and Stardust to the ranch. As they approached Hickory Trail Drive, an unidentified vehicle forced them off the road. Wendy was then forcibly abducted at gunpoint. Sherri reached the farm and immediately contacted her father, yet police intervention was inexplicably delayed until the following morning. The key witness to the initial altercation, Brian X, was subsequently murdered, alongside Detective Lois Pointer."

"And your proof?"

"Brian X wouldn't have been murdered if he hadn't witnessed the crime. And I wouldn't have been beaten to within an inch of my life if I hadn't uncovered the truth," I asserted firmly.

Ram turned to Rita. "Does Sheriff Tanner endorse this conjecture of Stone's?"

"Sir, the Sheriff deputised Mr Stone due to his conviction in the case," Rita replied cautiously.

"Well, I'm a firm believer in evaluation before belief ... there's no tangible evidence here, Stone ... Who are you implicating in the crime?"

"It was either Cowboy, members of his band, or your brother," I stated bluntly.

Ram's face reddened with anger. "You're accusing my brother of murdering my daughter, or suggesting her boyfriend might be involved ... and your only evidence is the beating you endured for meddling where you're unwelcome. You're wasting my fucking my time, boy."

Unfazed, I countered. "Two individuals who also believed in the truth were killed, not by the man currently imprisoned for murder, but by someone incensed by my investigations. That alone convinces me there's more beneath the surface. This was your daughter we're talking about. Why has critical evidence vanished? Why are you shielding your brother and Norton? Why hasn't there been an official disclosure about your daughter's murder?"

He stared at me with icy, predator-like eyes and said chillingly, "I could seal this aircraft, ascend to twenty-five thousand feet, and let you out ... Ponder on that, Stone."

I didn't waver. Standing up, I declared, "There's no merit in discussing this further with you, Ram." I made my way off the plane.

The silence in the car on our return to downtown was heavy and unbroken. Eventually, Rita cut through the stillness, her voice tinged with a mix of incredulity and concern, "Do you make a habit of antagonising influential figures?"

"Comes with the gig," I replied, my voice laced with a nonchalant acceptance of the hazards of my profession.

"And what's our next step?" she inquired, her voice a mix of curiosity and apprehension.

After a moment of reflection, I said, "A coffee first. Where can we find the best cup of Java in town?"

"Java?" Rita queried, a hint of amusement in her tone.

"Yeah, Java. It's what my dad used to call coffee. I suppose it's because he spent time in Java during WWII, and they grow coffee there. It stuck with me," I explained, a nostalgic edge creeping into my voice.

Rita nodded, a smile playing on her lips. "I know just the place. They roast their own beans, and the aroma is something else. Let's head there."

As Rita navigated the city streets, the tension from the encounter with Cyrus Ram began to dissolve, replaced by the mundane yet comforting task of seeking out a good cup of coffee. It was these small moments of normalcy that grounded me in the chaotic world of detective work.

~ ~ ~

Charlie had meticulously prepared the heads of agreement, poised for signatures. His task was to represent Serina Sun, while he awaited Gerri, acting on behalf of Kane Stevenson, to do likewise. The final step involved forwarding the document to Niko Yan for his endorsement, assuming no revisions were necessary. A preliminary version had been circulated via email to all parties, and thus far, it had been met without dissent.

Carmen, on the other hand, harboured reservations. She approached Charlie's desk, her expression etched with concern. "I recognise that look," Charlie remarked, his eyes briefly lifting from the paperwork.

"I'm uneasy about our role in handling Serina's affairs, especially with her agent being so unpredictable," Carmen confessed.

"In reality, the map is the linchpin of this agreement. Should it surface, we'll have grounds for renegotiation, particularly given potential involvement from entities like Pegasus," Charlie clarified.

"I understand, yet something feels off to me," Carmen replied, her disquiet lingering.

At that moment, Carol entered with an update. "Enzo just reported in ... Lucian Grange, Serina's agent, was scouring the house for the map."

"A testament to his erratic nature," Carmen observed, her anxiety underscored.

Gerri Jewel's voice echoed from the reception area, "Knock, knock."

"Come in, Gerri," Charlie invited.

Gerri, donning a vibrantly flamboyant outfit, infused the office with her colourful presence. "That ensemble is quite striking, Gerri," Charlie commented playfully.

Carmen, preoccupied with her concerns, found little amusement in Charlie's light-hearted exchange with Gerri.

As they congregated in the lounge, coffees in hand courtesy of Carol, business matters came to the fore. "Has Kane perused the agreement?" Charlie inquired.

"He's content with it, but now harbours apprehensions about the Yan family's awareness that the map remains undiscovered," Gerri disclosed.

"And the possibility of them attempting another theft," Carmen interjected.

"Precisely," Gerri concurred.

"God forbid if the treasure gets found then," Charlie put forward, his tone heavy with implication.

He was right, and they all knew it. The current level of paranoia was just the tip of the iceberg. If the multi-million-dollar treasure were to be unearthed, the situation would escalate from intolerable to potentially catastrophic.

"We've done all we can on this case," Charlie concluded, "It may be prudent to pass the baton to you."

Carmen appeared somewhat relieved, but Gerri was adamant. "No, Mr Chan, your involvement persists until the map's fate is conclusively determined."

"That seems unfair," Carmen remarked gently.

"You're correct, Gerri. We bear a responsibility," Charlie acknowledged.

"Kane also requests a comprehensive search for the map," Gerri added.

"Enzo's already on-site at the house," Charlie stated.

"Accompanied by Lucian Grange," Carmen pointed out.

"I'm wary of him after the media leak," Gerri admitted.

"He attributes that to Pegasus," Charlie noted.

Gerri raised an eyebrow conceding, "That wouldn't surprise me."

At that juncture, Enzo entered, looking utterly drained. "You look like you've endured a marathon," Gerri quipped.

"Worse than that," Enzo responded, his voice heavy with fatigue. "We've torn apart every nook of that house, relocated furniture, scoured every conceivable space … and found absolutely nothing." His frustration was evident, mirroring the exhaustive nature of their futile search.

"Did Grange help?" Carmen asked, her curiosity evident.

"He did, surprisingly hardworking," Enzo responded with an unexpected note of respect.

Carol, sensing a moment to lighten the mood, brought Enzo a chilled beer.

"You're an angel," he said gratefully, taking a deep sip of the cold brew.

"What's Niko Yan like?" Gerri inquired, her eyes fixed on Charlie.

"He's got the demeanour of every Hong Kong gangster I've ever encountered," Charlie confessed, a subtle undertone of unease in his voice.

"And believe me, he's met his fair share," Carmen added, her voice a blend of admiration and caution.

"To put it bluntly," Charlie elaborated, reflecting on his experience, "he's not someone you'd want to cross paths with in a dark alley, nor is he a man you'd wish as an adversary."

Gerri, intrigued by this description, wondered aloud, "In a deal like this, how can anyone trust someone like that?"

"You don't," Enzo cut in, his voice laced with experience. "I've heard Axis say, 'When you're at a crossroad, just keep going.'"

"That's classic Axis," Charlie agreed, a note of respect evident in his voice.

"I need to meet this Axis," Gerri declared, clearly fascinated. "He's your partner, right?"

"Yes, he's one hell of a PI," Charlie confirmed, his voice carrying a mix of pride and respect.

As they discussed a joint effort to re-examine the house the following day, Gerri made her departure. Charlie handed Carmen a glass of red wine and offered another beer to Enzo, then settled back to enjoy a drink at the day's end.

"With Gerri gone..." Enzo began, his voice hinting at a revelation, "I think I might know where the map is hidden."

Carmen's face brightened with anticipation. "Seriously? Where?"

Enzo laid out his theory: "Thing of it is, it has to be concealed either within the walls or beneath something predating the last sixty years. That rules out much of the house. The walls aren't double-cavity, and the attic's been remodelled into a bedroom. The marble entrance is barely twenty-five years old, and the garage is a recent addition." He paused for effect. "But, when we lifted the carpet in the main bedroom, we discovered newspapers used for insulation, dated December 22, 1981, decades after Knight's time."

"So, what's left?" Carmen leaned in, her excitement palpable.

"Well, there's an old built-in wardrobe in the attic, half for hanging clothes, half a chest of drawers. The chest is removable, and beneath it lies a patch of the original carpet."

"Under the carpet!" Charlie exclaimed, realisation dawning.

Carmen, barely containing her excitement, blurted out, "Did you check there?"

"Not with Grange around," Enzo confessed. "I didn't mention it to him. I think we should go back tonight to check it out. Serina's staying at the Mondrian, and Grange is clueless. We might just uncover the map and then decide our next move."

Raising his glass, Charlie toasted, "To a night of discovery."

CHAPTER
ELEVEN

Seething with anger, I was more convinced than ever after meeting Cyrus Ram that the entire case was contaminated. Cyrus, undoubtedly a criminal, exhibited traits typical of the felonious minds I'd encountered throughout my career. He was the epicentre of this turmoil, and the pressing question now was his ultimate motive. Engulfed in these thoughts, I was only vaguely aware as Rita drove us through town. Her earlier caution about creating powerful adversaries resonated in my mind. Her phone rang just as she parked in front of L&L Market in West Nashville.

We walked into the mall and entered Honest Coffee Roasters café. I sat at a bench, scanning the menu while Rita concluded her call.

"What are you having?" she inquired after disconnecting the call.

"The Bootlegger," I responded, still partially preoccupied with my thoughts.

Rita placed our orders and, upon returning, sat opposite me, her expression serious. "That was Lieutenant Way from CSI. He confirmed the tyre tracks at the crime scene match Beano Curtis's car, and they've found blood in the vehicle. They're now verifying if it matches Wendy Ram's DNA."

This was the breakthrough I had been waiting for.

"Your theory seems increasingly plausible," Rita observed, her face lighting up as our coffees arrived.

I took a sip of my coffee, a perfect fusion of espresso, milk, and homemade bourbon caramel syrup. "Top-notch Java, just what I needed," I commented, relishing the temporary reprieve.

"I opted for the same," Rita said, smiling.

Setting my mug down, my mind pivoted back to the case. "So, we've pinpointed the vehicle involved in the abduction. Our next step is to scrutinise CCTV footage that might track the car. Sherri and the others mentioned it made a U-turn and headed back into town. Let's start with the surveillance at Johnny Ram's car dealership," I proposed, my mind already strategizing the upcoming phase of our investigation.

Invigorated by the caffeine, we swiftly headed to the car. "Time to have a chat with the Sheriff," I stated resolutely.

"I'll focus on the CCTV footage," Rita responded, her determination matching mine.

Fifteen minutes later, I was sitting across from Sheriff Tanner in his office, acutely aware of the need for tact in discussing Cyrus Ram, sensing an uncomfortably close tie between them.

"It seems you've agitated Cyrus Ram," Sheriff Tanner started sternly, his gaze fixed on me.

"I didn't go there to win friends. My inquiries were bound to stir a reaction. He's been in touch with you, I presume?" I replied, trying to read his expression.

"Yes, he called. Gave me an earful. Thinks your theory is rubbish," the Sheriff stated bluntly.

"Well, then he's not going to appreciate the next bit of 'trash' I have to deliver." I watched as his previously confident demeanour faltered, and he leaned forward with interest.

"Oh yeah? What's that?" he asked, his curiosity piqued.

"The CSI team has confirmed the tyre tracks at the crime scene match Beano Curtis's vehicle, the same one Travis Norton used on the night he confronted Wendy outside The Local. I'm bringing in Norton and the Curtis brothers for questioning."

The Sheriff leaned back, twirling a pen between his fingers, a sign of contemplation. "That's standard procedure," he admitted, though with evident reluctance.

"Additionally, I plan to arrest Johnny Ram on suspicion of the murders of Detective Pointer and Brian X."

The Sheriff's reaction was sceptical. "Good luck with that, son. Don't expect any cooperation—you'll face resistance."

"So be it," I said, my tone resolute.

He raised an eyebrow. "You realise you don't have sufficient evidence to detain him, right?"

"I'm confident the necessary evidence will emerge from Norton and the Curtis brothers. They're all deeply entangled in this," I stated, certain that the truth would soon unravel.

Standing up, ready to leave his office, I paused at the door, turning back. "And Eo?" I asked, the name laden with significance.

"He's staying put," the Sheriff answered dismissively, his tone final.

"On what grounds? I've provided substantial evidence for his exoneration," I pressed, my frustration mounting.

"The courts will decide," he responded coldly, his face impassive.

I stepped closer, our eyes locked in a silent confrontation. "You need to drop the charges against him," I urged firmly.

"I don't 'need' to do anything," he retorted coldly, his gaze icy.

"How do you sleep, knowing an innocent man is incarcerated?" I challenged, appalled at his indifference.

"Like a baby. Is that all?" he shot back, his attitude unyielding.

Incensed, I left his office and immediately called Rita. She was engrossed in analysing traffic CCTV footage at the Traffic and Parking Commission. After updating her on the Sheriff's obstinacy, I left her to her crucial task and headed to the Downtown Detention Center to visit Eo.

At the detention center, I confidently displayed my badge and, with some firm persuasion, convinced the guards to check with Sheriff Tanner's office about my visitation rights. I opted not to involve defence attorney Reece, preferring to rely on my own authority. My approach paid off, and I was granted permission to see Eo.

Eo's appearance was disheartening; he seemed a mere shadow of his former self. I endeavoured to lift his spirits, sharing the latest positive developments and expressing my firm belief in his imminent release. Eo's concern for the girls at the commune was evident, and I regretted not having visited them since my initial trip to the ranch. Despite my offers of assistance, he declined, so I left him with a commitment to check on the girls soon. I resolved to have attorney Reece negotiate with the State prosecutor tomorrow about releasing Eo on his own recognisance or on bail.

As I left the detention center, my thoughts were swirling. Back in my hotel room, I poured a shot of JD into a glass, the day's events replaying in my mind. A quick glance at my phone informed me that The Haybale Rollers were playing tonight at The Basement. This presented an ideal chance to confront Norton and the rest of the band and demand their presence at the Sheriff's office the following morning.

~ ~ ~

Carmen had vehemently opposed Enzo and Charlie's clandestine mission to uncover the map, but her protests were in vain. Despite the signed agreement between all parties, they proceeded with their plan.

Cloaked in the guise of cat burglars, they approached the house, shrouded by the dense darkness of the night. Once inside, amidst the disarray, they disabled the alarm system and ascended towards the narrow corridor leading to the attic stairs. Enzo flicked on his torch, its beam slicing through the pervading darkness. Just as they were about to mount the attic stairs, a sound from below halted them. Quickly, Enzo switched off the torch, and they listened intently.

"Someone's ascending the stairs. Hurry..." Charlie whispered.

They darted into the main bedroom. Behind the half-open bedroom door, he listened. A creak of floorboards betrayed the interloper, who was creeping along the corridor towards the staircase to the attic. Enzo turned to Charlie, his eyes and mouth visible through the black balaclava, and pointed up towards the attic to let Charlie know the intruder was headed for the same location as them.

Charlie pointed for Enzo to 'go'.

Gun drawn, Enzo stepped into the hallway, confronting the shadowy figure. "Stop right there," he commanded.

The figure obeyed, hands raised.

"Turn around. Remove your balaclava," Enzo instructed. The figure complied, revealing Gerri Jewel's distinct blonde hair.

"Gerri?" Charlie voiced in astonishment.

"Charlie? Is that you?" Gerri responded, equally surprised.

Enzo turned on the torch, and Charlie removed his balaclava. Their unexpected reunion was cut short by additional sounds from downstairs. Swiftly, they retreated to their hiding place in the bedroom as new figures ascended the stairs.

The newcomers, made their way very quickly up the staircase and into the corridor. Enzo, torch in one hand and gun in the other, stepped out to confront them. The light revealed Serina Sun and her agent, Lucian Grange, who instinctively raised their hands to shield their eyes from the bright beam.

"Serina? Lucian? What on earth are you doing here?" Enzo inquired, visibly taken aback by their presence.

"I live here, stupid. Get that torch out of my eyes, Enzo; you'll give me myopia," Serina retorted sharply.

As Charlie and Gerri emerged alongside Enzo, Serina remarked sarcastically, "What is this, a party?"

Lucian suddenly turned back towards the main staircase, then back at Enzo and whispered, "There's someone downstairs!" Enzo flicked off the torch.

Charlie gestured for everyone to hide in the bedroom. Now crowded with five individuals, the bedroom was tense, with Enzo stationed at the door, listening intently. Charlie was about to whisper to Enzo when Enzo signalled for silence; the distinct creaking of floorboards indicated the presence of others. He held up three fingers to indicate the number of new arrivals.

Enzo decided to let them pass, but this time, their approach was different. The bedroom door slowly creaked open, revealing a dark figure stepping inside. Enzo's torch suddenly illuminated Niko Yan, a gun in his hand.

"Niko?" Charlie questioned in disbelief.

Niko, gun trained on Charlie, was followed by two accomplices. Enzo switched on the bedroom light, and a tense stand-off ensued before all parties lowered their weapons, realising the sheer absurdity of the situation.

"Okay," Charlie said, breaking the silence, "it seems we're all here, ignoring the agreement in search of the map."

Gerri chimed in with dry humour, "Not exactly setting a great example, are we?"

"We agreed to a coordinated search," Niko stated flatly.

Charlie lightened the mood with a joke, "Is anyone missing?"

"Only Kane Stevenson," Gerri replied.

Taking control of the situation, Charlie asked, "Niko, where do you think the map is?"

"Right here, obviously," Niko responded.

"And your thoughts, Gerri?"

"I planned to start from the top and work my way down."

Turning to Serina and Grange, Charlie inquired, "Grange, you were here earlier with Enzo?"

"I believe it's in the attic," Grange asserted confidently. "Enzo knows what I mean, right?"

Enzo, removing his balaclava, remained tight-lipped. Charlie now faced a pivotal decision: be forthcoming about their true intentions or maintain the facade to secure the map for themselves.

~ ~ ~

After waking up, surrounded by empty miniatures from the minibar, I answered the ringing phone. "Hey, Rita, how'd you go?" I asked, still groggy.

"Did I wake you?" Rita sounded apologetic.

"I was just catching forty winks…" I replied, trying to shake off the sleep.

"I've got something," Rita announced, her voice tinged with excitement. "Beano's car was seen entering downtown Nashville via Interstate 40, coming from the direction of Hickory Trail Drive. It had a couple of blind spots but was spotted going into Johnny Ram's second-hand car yard at exactly 12.05 am. It left at 12.35 am and headed straight to the house on Hillside Avenue, rented by the Curtis brothers and Travis Norton. I couldn't see who was in or out of the car, though."

"That's good enough for me," I responded, adrenaline kicking in. "Tie all that information together, and we'll confront them with it in the morning."

"Have you spoken to them yet?" Rita inquired.

"No, I'm going to catch them tonight at The Basement after their gig," I said.

"What time are they on?"

"They start at 8.30. I reckon they'll do a forty-five-minute set," I guessed.

"I expect so. I can't pick you up at the Conrad, but I can meet you at The Basement. It's close to where I live. See you there around 9."

"Oki-doki." I hung up, feeling a sense of purpose renewed.

I had hoped to visit the girls at the ranch tonight, but it had been a long day. That visit would have to wait until tomorrow. Now, I needed to focus on catching up with the band at The Basement.

It was 8 pm in New York, so I decided to call Patricia. Her reaction to hearing about my recent beating and the additional murders was understandably fraught with worry.

"You should get Charlie to come give you a hand ... you helped him out in Hong Kong when he was in a tight spot," she suggested, her concern palpable.

"I'll be fine. Like I said, I've been deputised. I've got the police force backing me now," I reassured her, downplaying the danger.

"From what you've said about that Sheriff, I'm not sure if that's a help or a hindrance," she countered, clearly unconvinced. "Next thing you know, you'll have the KKK after you."

"I hope not," I said, attempting to lighten the mood. "Anyway, I hear you. This should all be wrapped up soon. My duty ends once Eo is released from jail."

"Eo? I thought it was David Bowie?"

"Ziggy Stardust, that's his stage name. His real name is Eo," I clarified.

"Eo what? He must have a surname. How am I supposed to look him up without a last name?"

"True. So, what's happening on your end?"

"I talked to Carmen earlier. She thinks they'll close their case in a day or two. Kendy's been busy with exams. And I've been missing you ... and fending off advances from the vibrator in your dresser."

"Whose is that?" I asked, a bit taken aback.

"No idea, it was in your underwear drawer."

"That sounds like a mystery I'll need to investigate seriously when I get back."

"I'll note it in your diary," she joked.

"Oki doki, I better get something to eat to fuel up for tonight's adventure."

"I've had half a dozen calls for our services."

"Good to know we're in demand," I said, "take care, I miss you."

"Bye, baby. Be careful."

I hung up, feeling a mix of gratitude and love. How lucky I was to have someone like Patricia in my life. With renewed resolve, I prepared for the night ahead at The Basement.

The realisation that I hadn't seen Wendy Ram's death certificate suddenly struck me as odd, especially since it wasn't included in the police report provided by attorney Reece. I quickly texted Rita, requesting her to obtain a copy from Dr Vickerman, the medical examiner.

CHAPTER
TWELVE

After dining in my room, still looking like a losing prizefighter post-bout, I dressed for the night at The Basement. Concealing my battered eyes with sunglasses, I stepped out to hail a taxi.

The Basement, a vibrant venue housed in a 106-year-old red brick building with '1604' prominently displayed on its façade, was quiet outside—typical for a Wednesday night. Inside, however, the atmosphere was pulsating with life. I paid the entry and navigated through the bar area, sparsely populated with patrons, to the concert room below. The Haybale Rollers were setting up on the stage, level with the audience, promising an intimate gig. The room buzzed with about eighty to a hundred people. I found a seat at the back, intrigued by the band's reputation and recalling that even Metallica had played in this very room.

Cowboy, exuding the charm of a seasoned country rock star, led the band. Their opening number, 'Rainy Day Blues,' was a mellow track that unexpectedly revealed their musical depth, contradicting my earlier assumptions about Cowboy's band.

Meanwhile, Rita, on her way to The Basement, received a call from Sheriff Tanner.

"Suarez, where are you?" he asked sharply.

"En route to The Basement to meet Stone," she replied. "Sir, I've tracked Beano's car. It was at the crime scene of Wendy Ram's murder."

"And after?"

"It went to Johnny Ram's car yard, then to Hillside Avenue," Rita informed him.

"Did you tell Stone?"

"Yes, sir."

"Alright, here's what I need you to do..." Tanner began, outlining his instructions to Rita.

Back at The Basement, as the band's set unfolded, I kept an eye out for Rita. She hadn't shown up by the end of the gig, and my concern grew. My calls to her went straight to voicemail. I left a message, urging her to call back as soon as possible.

Resolved to move forward with the plan, I made my way backstage, bypassing security with my badge. There, I ran into Cowboy as he was exiting.

"Cowboy, we need to talk," I said.

"What's up, man?" he asked, an edge of wariness in his voice.

"I need you and the Curtis brothers at the Sheriff's office, 11 am tomorrow," I informed him, my tone professional yet firm.

"What for?" he asked, his defensiveness apparent.

"Questions about the night Wendy Ram was murdered," I explained, showing my badge.

"Why not now?" Cowboy challenged.

"It needs to be official. Are Beano and Raddo still here?" I inquired.

"Yeah," he responded shortly, then turned and left.

I entered the dressing room, finding Beano and Raddo. With the same authoritative stance, I informed them of the need to appear at the Sheriff's office the following morning. As they registered the gravity of the situation, it was clear that the next day would bring significant developments in the case.

~ ~ ~

In the confined space of the tiny attic, the air was charged with tension as our group of eight huddled together. The moment of truth had arrived. With some effort, Enzo opened the wardrobe door and slid out the chest of drawers. Kneeling down, he gripped the edge of an old carpet, hidden beneath the drawers. Peeling it back, layers of newspaper came into view.

"The newspaper is dated April 2, 1967," Enzo announced, scanning the faded print. "Front page of The Times, headline reads: 'A Halt to Bombing of North Vietnam Proposed.'"

"Enough with the history, Enzo, just get on with it," Grange interjected, unable to hide his impatience.

Ignoring Grange, Enzo carefully removed the newspaper, revealing a hidden compartment beneath. We all leaned in, our breaths held in anticipation, as Enzo reached into the space. After a moment, he turned to face us, a triumphant look in his eyes.

"What is it?" Selina's voice quivered with excitement.

In a grand gesture, Enzo held up his find, declaring, "It's a treasure map."

The atmosphere in the attic escalated instantly as Niko, quick as a flash, drew a gun and pointed it at Enzo. "I'll take that," he demanded, his eyes locked onto the map.

Before the situation could spiral out of control, Gerri quickly drew her own weapon, aiming it at Niko. "Not so fast," she asserted confidently.

Charlie, reacting with quick thinking to the escalating situation, also drew his gun and aimed it at Niko. His voice was calm and authoritative, contrasting with the fraught moment. "Let's put away the hardware and talk this over," he suggested, trying to deescalate the situation.

The room was instantly caught in a classic Mexican standoff, each participant wary and on edge. The air was thick with suspense, every move calculated and fraught with potential consequences. The treasure map lay at the centre of this delicate balance of power, its discovery having transformed the attic from a mere cramped and dusty space into a critical battleground.

This attic, steeped in the dark past where Knight had been

tortured and murdered by Niko's mother, Luo Yan, now hosted a new chapter of confrontation. The same space that had witnessed Knight's final moments after hiding the map was now the arena for a showdown that could dramatically alter the course of events. The tension was almost palpable, each participant keenly aware of the stakes at hand in this climactic moment.

~ ~ ~

As I savoured my eggs Benedict at the Blue Aster, Rita's unexpected arrival caught me off guard. Her troubled expression signalled something serious.

"Hey Rita, sit down. Want something to eat?" I gestured to the seat opposite me.

She sat, looking deeply concerned. "Just coffee, please. There's a problem, Axis."

I signalled for a server to bring her coffee. "What's going on? Is this about you not showing up last night?"

"Yes, that, and more," she leaned in, lowering her voice. "Sheriff Tanner called me on my way to meet you. He explicitly told me not to join you."

"Why would he do that?" I asked, perplexed by the Sheriff's interference.

Rita sighed, frustration in her tone. "I don't know. I couldn't just ignore his order, but I knew you could handle things."

"It's okay, Rita. I understand," I reassured her, sensing her conflict. "Was he worried about us arresting Johnny Ram?"

"I think so," she nodded. "Maybe thinking that was on, he'd warned him."

I paused, considering the implications. "What else? You said there was more."

"There is." Rita's voice was grave as she handed me a document. "You wanted Wendy Ram's death certificate, right? Well, it doesn't exist. I talked to Dr Vickerman. This autopsy report is for a Jane Doe, not Wendy, and it's signed by an unknown assistant."

I leaned back, contemplating the revelation. "Do you realise what this means, Rita?"

She shook her head, her eyes reflecting confusion and concern. "No, what?"

"Wendy Ram isn't dead," I stated bluntly, the words heavy with implication.

The realisation slowly dawned on her. "So Eo is being falsely imprisoned?"

"Exactly. The secrecy, the lack of press coverage—it's all orchestrated. The Sheriff and Cyrus Ram are conspiring to discredit Eo and protect Ram's campaign."

"But how could they sustain that?" Rita asked, her voice laced with incredulity.

"They can't, not for long. They'd release Eo post-election, intimidate him into silence, and the girls would resurface. Wendy's probably hidden away safely."

"And the murders of Brian X and Detective Pointer?"

"My guess? Johnny Ram was tasked with silencing Brian but couldn't manage it. Brian was not the type to be easily intimidated or controlled. In a fit of rage, Johnny likely went too far and killed him. As for Pointer, she was simply in the wrong place at the wrong time."

"So, who took Wendy?"

"I bet on Cowboy, coerced by Cyrus or Johnny, but not to harm her. If I hadn't intervened, they might have succeeded. My involvement escalated things."

Our coffee arrived as we absorbed the gravity of the situation.

"We'll see what unfolds at 11 am when Cowboy and the others are due for questioning," I mused.

"You think they won't show," Rita said, scepticism in her voice.

"I doubt they will. Then we can arrest Johnny Ram and free Eo. Job done. Thanks for trusting me, Rita."

"That's what the badge is for," she replied solemnly.

"I've been meaning to ask, with the name Suarez, is your heritage Spanish?"

She smiled faintly. "I'm Choctaw, from Lauderdale County. My birth name is Tula, meaning 'mountain peak.'"

Her response revealed a depth I hadn't fully appreciated. From then on, I resolved to call her Tula.

Arriving at the Sheriff's office felt akin to being summoned to the principal's office as a schoolboy. The office exuded an intimidating atmosphere; chairs were conspicuously absent from in front of the Sheriff's desk, lined up against the wall instead, compelling us to stand—a gesture I interpreted as either an attempt to humiliate or a display of dominance.

"What evidence do you have to bring in Norton and the Curtis brothers?" Sheriff Tanner asked sharply.

"The tyre tracks, sir. I'm sure you..." I began, only to be cut off.

"That's not sufficient," he interjected briskly.

"There's also the CCTV, showing the vehicle traveling to and from the crime scene," I persisted.

"Is that conclusive, Detective Suarez?" he questioned, his scepticism apparent.

"Yes, sir. The plates match," Rita affirmed confidently.

"It's not strong enough to reopen the case," the Sheriff dismissed our argument.

"I didn't realise it needed reopening ... If there's reasonable doubt about Eo's guilt, then..." I tried to argue.

He interrupted again, "The court will decide that. Your services here are no longer needed, Stone," he said flatly.

"I beg to differ, Sheriff. My client decides that," I countered, my resolve unwavering, which seemed to irk him further.

"You're no longer deputised, Stone. Go home," he declared definitively.

I placed my badge on his desk. "No problem, Sheriff. Thank you for your patience. I assume Norton and the Curtis brothers won't be questioned?"

"You got that right," he confirmed reluctantly.

"And you won't release Eo, aka Ziggy Stardust?"

"Correct."

I nodded, acknowledging his position, and headed towards the door. Pausing, I turned back. "I'll be leaving today, after speaking with a reporter from The Tennessean."

I reached for the door when the Sheriff called out, "Hold on, Stone."

I stopped, closed the door, and faced him again.

"What will you tell this reporter?" he inquired, a trace of anxiety in his voice.

"I'll say Wendy Ram isn't dead, she's held somewhere until after the election. That Eo is wrongly accused and jailed. And that evidence in the murders of Brian X and Detective Pointer is being suppressed."

The ensuing silence was profound. The Sheriff paled, while Rita gave me a subtle, approving glance.

Before he could respond, I added, "Of course, this can be avoided if you agree to arrest Johnny Ram for the murders and release Eo immediately."

The ball was now squarely in his court, the stakes higher than ever.

CHAPTER
THIRTEEN

As Tula and I strolled towards her car, she couldn't help but remark on the audacity of my manoeuvre in the Sheriff's office. "That was quite a bold move," she said, her voice laced with a hint of admiration.

I responded with a slight grin, trying to lighten the mood. "My friends call me kemosabe," I quipped.

Her laughter, a welcome relief in the midst of our grave circumstances, echoed around us.

Clutching my deputy badge, a symbol of the renewed authority bestowed upon me, I stated resolutely, "Let's go bring in Johnny Ram."

~ ~ ~

In the Californian sunshine, Carmen relaxed in her deckchair by the pool, turning her attention to Charlie. "Handing out copies of the map to everyone was a smart move, hon," she said, her voice laced with laziness and contentment.

Charlie, sipping his coffee while admiring the view from their patio on Doheny Drive, nodded thoughtfully. "It was the only way to stop them from tearing each other apart over it."

"And getting Niko to agree to redo Serina's house? That was clever," Carmen added, acknowledging his strategic acumen.

Charlie mused over the situation. "It'll be interesting to see if they can work together on a joint venture to find the treasure."

Carmen, peering over her sunglasses, teased, "I thought you'd want in on that hunt."

Charlie replied, a hint of mystery in his tone, "Just watch this space ... Hong Kong might become a key player, and we've got an office there."

"Oh, because the island is..." Carmen led on, prompting him.

"The Vietnamese island of Phu Quoc, in the Gulf of Thailand. About 200 miles west of Ho Chi Minh City," Charlie elaborated. "Heard the fishing there is excellent."

Carmen gave him a warning glance. "You're not seriously considering treasure hunting, are you, Charlie Chan?"

He looked at her playfully, a twinkle in his eye. "Might discuss it with Axis and Nick. Axis nearly found a treasure at Lindos Estate, remember? And Nick ... well..."

"Over my dead body, Charlie Chan," Carmen interjected firmly.

Charlie, pretending to be mischievous, said, "That can be arranged," and chuckled.

"You wouldn't want to go after Captain Kidd's treasure," Carmen warned.

"And why not, ma'am?" he asked, intrigued.

"Because you're about to get a Kidd of your own," she hinted, her voice tinged with mystery.

Charlie paused, then it dawned on him. "Ah! That explains the mood swings and morning paleness!"

"Yes, darling, I'm growing a belly-full of arms and legs," Carmen confirmed with a broad, joyful grin.

In an instant, Charlie set aside the map and leaped from his chair to embrace her. "Were you waiting for the detective in me to figure it out?"

"I most certainly have," she confessed, her smile widening. They kissed passionately, celebrating this new, thrilling chapter in their lives.

~ ~ ~

As Tula and I headed toward Ram Motors, the anticipation inside me was palpable. This was my chance to confront Johnny Ram, the man I suspected was behind the brutal attack I had suffered and the deaths of Detective Pointer and Brian X.

Pulling into the car lot, we stepped out and made our way toward the office building. It wasn't surprising to find that Johnny Ram wasn't there. Tula asked about his whereabouts and was informed that he was at his ranch in Franklin, about forty minutes south of Nashville.

Exiting the car lot, I proposed, "Let's call his ranch to confirm he's there. Someone from here is likely tipping him off right now."

Tula nodded in agreement and suggested, "I'll get the Franklin police to keep him there until we arrive," as she reached for her phone.

"Good idea," I concurred.

While Tula made the necessary arrangements, I called Charlie to check in. He shared updates about his case and the thrilling prospect of searching for Captain Kidd's treasure, which genuinely intrigued me. The icing on the cake was hearing about their expected baby. I shared my progress with him, mentioning that I expected to wrap up my case in a day or two. As I ended the call, Tula informed me that the Franklin police were already on their way to Ram's ranch to ensure he stayed put until we arrived.

The drive to Johnny Ram's ranch was marked by a tense silence. Tula and I were both deep in thought, preparing ourselves for what might await us. The ranch itself was a stark contrast to the task at hand. Nestled in a lush green valley with the Harpeth River meandering through, it was more of a serene hideaway than a working farm. The sprawling two-storey timber manor house exuded a sense of peace, belying the turmoil that was about to unfold.

As we neared the ranch, the sight of a police car parked out front was expected. However, the discovery of two motionless officers on the ground indicated the severity of the situation. "Stop," I instructed

Tula urgently, and she brought the car to a skidding halt.

We approached cautiously, guns drawn, using the police car as cover. The grim reality struck us— the officers were dead, their bodies riddled with bullet holes. I whispered to Tula, "Cover me." She was surprisingly composed under the circumstances. I dashed toward the slightly open front door and burst inside, shouting, "Police!" The response was a deafening silence. My calls for Johnny Ram to surrender were met with the same eerie quiet until the roar of a powerful V8 engine from the back of the house broke the silence.

As I sprinted out the front door, my legs protesting from the recent beating, I saw the 1973 red Corvette Stingray, previously spotted at Ram Motors, speeding down the driveway. Reaching Tula at the car, I heard her prompt, "Jump in, let's go!"

"No mate, phone the patrol cops; we'll never catch that thing. I'm going back in to search the house," I decided, knowing our chances of catching the Corvette were slim. We needed to gather any evidence we could find inside.

Tula quickly called the Franklin police to update them on the situation as I re-entered the house. The ground floor revealed nothing unusual, so I headed upstairs. In the main bedroom, I found an unmade king-size bed. After a careful search of the closet and bathroom, I moved on to the next room.

The smaller bedroom presented a different scene—another unmade bed, suggesting recent occupancy. As I investigated, a sudden noise made me whirl around, gun drawn. Relief washed over me as I saw Tula—it was just her.

In silence, she gestured for me to follow her into the en-suite bathroom. "Axis?" she whispered.

"What is it?" I joined her, curious.

"A woman has been staying here. The makeup mess suggests a teenager," she deduced.

"Wendy," I concluded instantly.

"Definitely," Tula agreed.

It was clear now; Johnny had fled with Wendy. We rushed back to the car, my mind swirling with the implications of this revelation. Tula confirmed she had informed the Franklin police about the officers and requested CSI to verify Wendy's presence in the house. The case was rapidly unfolding, and we were at the heart of it.

~ ~ ~

Charlie entered the office that morning, his thoughts lingering on Carmen who had stayed behind for a doctor's appointment. To his surprise, Gerri was in the reception, deep in conversation with Carol. Curious about her unanticipated visit, he invited Gerri into his office for a private chat in the lounge area.

"I wanted to update you on our talks with Niko. You're still representing Serina, aren't you?" Gerri inquired, cutting straight to the chase.

Charlie, acknowledging the situation's complexities, confirmed his ongoing involvement. "Things are a bit muddled with her agent now, but yes, let's assume I am for the sake of this discussion."

Gerri delved into the details. "Kane has rejected the exorbitant amount Niko demanded for the rights to use the family history in his screenplay. Without that, the project's basically dead in the water."

Charlie was surprised. "I thought intertwining Richard Knight's 60s adventures with our modern map hunt in a Hollywood star's home would be appealing."

Gerri shook her head. "No, the studios are keener on the gangster angle—Zhang Yan's demise and Luo Yan's escape to America."

"Isn't that public record?" Charlie asked.

"Yes, but Luo Yan's involvement isn't, and that's crucial for the American audience. It links the story between Hong Kong and the U.S."

Charlie nodded, understanding. "So, what's your plan?"

"Kane wants you to negotiate. Your knowledge of the culture and language..."

"My Cantonese is rusty," Charlie interjected with a smile.

Gerri smiled back. "Still, we think you'd do better than us. The studio will cover your expenses. What do you say?"

"I'll talk with my team and get back to you today," Charlie said, contemplating the proposal.

Gerri then asked about Carmen.

Charlie's face lit up with the news he'd received that morning. "She's at the doctor. Turns out, I'm going to be a dad."

Gerri's face brightened. "A little Chan-ette! Congratulations, Charlie."

After Gerri left, Charlie asked Carol to set up a meeting with Niko Yan. It was arranged for 7 pm at the Merois in West Hollywood.

As the day waned, Charlie realised how swiftly time had passed. The office had emptied, and he had just fifteen minutes to get to the Merois. Conveniently located along Sunset Boulevard, he was confident he'd arrive on time. His phone rang; it was Enzo.

"Enzo, what's up?"

"Lucian Grange called, upset about the screenplay deal falling through."

"I'm headed to meet Niko about that. They couldn't agree on the rights fee."

"Always tricky, those rights issues. Need help?"

"No, thanks. Let's catch up tomorrow. Where are you?"

"At dinner with Carol."

"On a date?"

"Yeah, my first in a while."

"Have a good one."

At the Merois, Charlie quickly settled in and started perusing the menu. He looked up to see Niko already seated across from him.

"Hey, Niko. Didn't see you come in."

"I don't have much time. I have a flight to Hong Kong. What do you need?"

"I'm here to mediate a deal with you. What's the sticking point?"

Niko removed his sunglasses and fixed Charlie with a penetrating gaze. "The filmmakers want to use our family history for a share of the box office takings. That's acceptable, but we want an upfront payment."

"Did they reject an advance, or was the offer too low?"

"They agreed to pay after securing the budget. That's not good enough."

"I see. How about treating it like an option, like with novels? A fair upfront sum, an option for a year, and if they secure funding, you get the rest. Plus, an executive producer credit and a share of profits."

"What's your number?"

"What did you ask for?"

"A million upfront."

In Cantonese, Charlie proposed a more feasible deal: two hundred thousand upfront, three hundred thousand from development funds, and half a million upon budget approval, plus five percent of net profits.

Switching back to English, Niko wanted ten percent.

Aware that bargaining was customary, Charlie suggested six; Niko countered with eight. They settled on seven percent.

Niko stood up. "No time to dine." He raised a glass of water in a toast. "Gōn bāi."

"Gōn bāi," Charlie responded, their glasses clinking in agreement.

Having dined alone, Charlie stepped out and called Gerri. The call went to voicemail, so he left a message about the deal with Niko. Soon after, Gerri texted him, asking for a meeting at her apartment on Kings Road in West Hollywood.

Charlie arrived at Gerri's place, knocking on the door. It opened to reveal Gerri with damp hair, dressed in a string bikini under a translucent kimono. "Hi Charlie, come in. I just need to change," she said, having just returned from a swim.

"I can't stay long," Charlie quickly said, stopping her from going to the bedroom.

"Let me get you a drink at least. JD on ice, right?"

As she moved to prepare the drinks, Charlie's gaze lingered on her alluring figure, barely concealed by the flimsy kimono.

"So, you met with Niko?"

"Yes, he's off to Hong Kong tonight."

She returned with their drinks, clinked glasses in a toast, and then settled opposite him. Charlie's eyes couldn't help but drift to her bronzed legs and meticulously pedicured feet in their elegant sandals.

Gerri asked, "Did he mention why he's going?"

"No, but I suspect it's to start preparations for a venture in Phu Quoc, searching for Kidd's treasure."

Gerri noticed Charlie's attention to her legs and subtly adjusted her position, enhancing his view. He sensed her openness to a more intimate interaction, a feeling that was mutual, yet he knew he had to resist. To shift the increasingly charged atmosphere, Charlie steered the conversation towards the deal he'd negotiated with Niko.

"I think Kane and the studio will accept these terms," Gerri opined. "But there might be concerns about Niko getting ahead in the treasure hunt."

Charlie inquired why.

"If Niko informs the Vietnamese authorities, they might block other expeditions," she explained.

"I see," he responded, his attention briefly shifting to her cleavage before he quickly stood up, finishing his drink.

"We'll talk more tomorrow. Let me know Kane's response," Charlie said, heading for the door.

Gerri followed him to the door, her hand on the knob. As she moved closer, the scent of her perfume was intoxicating. She leaned in, seemingly for a peck on the cheek, but at the last moment, their lips met in a fervent kiss, their mutual desire palpable. Her hand reached for him, a gesture he knew was as far as he was willing to go. Swiftly, he grabbed the door handle and pulled it open. They paused, their eyes locked, each contemplating what they were potentially forgoing, before Charlie walked away.

CHAPTER
FOURTEEN

Charlie found Carmen asleep on the couch, the television murmuring in the background. He poured two glasses of red wine and sat beside her, gently rousing her. Her eyes fluttered open, revealing a warm smile and she offered a tender kiss. She took the glass he offered, and they clinked in a toast.

"Here's to a successful deal," Charlie said.

"What deal?" Carmen inquired, sipping her wine.

Charlie recounted the negotiation process with Niko, carefully omitting his final encounter with Gerri. Carmen seemed pleased with the outcome, but her tone suddenly shifted to one of playful sarcasm.

"You're wearing a rather distinct perfume, hon."

Charlie tried to dismiss her comment casually.

"That's Phlur Missing Person Eau de Parfum. I recognise it," she said with a hint of jest, but her tone soon took on a more serious edge. Placing her glass down, she touched her barely noticeable pregnant belly. "I can't really indulge in wine now, and I'd suggest you refrain from wearing women's perfume."

With that, she stood up and left for the bedroom, leaving Charlie sitting alone, feeling both embarrassed and regretful.

~ ~ ~

Tula informed me that the all-points bulletin (APB) issued for Johnny Ram had not yielded any results; he seemed to have disappeared. She then escalated the search by requesting a state-wide APB, which was quickly approved due to the involvement of two police fatalities.

After the arrival of the police and Crime Scene Investigation (CSI) at the ranch, we headed back to Nashville. We were about twenty minutes into our drive when I received an anonymous call. Suspecting it might be Johnny Ram, I put it on speaker.

"Stone, Cyrus Ram here. We got off on the wrong foot. I want to make amends," he said in his Tennessee drawl.

"You heard about my threat to go to the press?"

"Yes. What started as a scare tactic for Ziggy Stardust spiralled out of control. I wanted my daughter back, like Tanner."

"I'm here to find Wendy and bring Johnny to justice. He's now responsible for four murders."

"Johnny's always been trouble. I protected him all his life, bought him the ranch and the business, but he and I are opposites. He's had mental issues in the past, booze, drugs, the wrong company, you know the drill ... and, I'm afraid they've worsened. I've tried to help him, but he's beyond my control now."

"Your daughter's in danger. Where would Johnny go?"

"He wouldn't hurt her..."

"But she could be caught in a shootout."

"I see what you're saying."

"Look, getting to him before a whole team of SWAT police find him gives Wendy a greater chance of making it through this ... Where is he?"

"I'm just thinking. There's a fishing lodge that belongs to the family up on Hidden Lake, you take Charlotte..."

"I know the way," Tula said. "What's the address?"

"4022 Hidden Lake Road ... But be real careful, it's well concealed and Johnny will be armed"

"We'll go there, but you get Sheriff Tanner to release Stardust. No confirmation, no discretion."

"You have my word and thanks. Please keep Wendy safe."

"Do you think he'll do it?" Tula asked.

"He has little choice, but we'll see."

Soon after, I received a text from Cyrus confirming Stardust's release.

"Was that the confirmation?" Tula asked.

"Yes, a victory for us."

Tula's phone rang. After a brief conversation, she shared, "Good news. My grandfather, Lone Running Wolf, is trialling an aged-care robot, ElliQ. I applied on his behalf about six months ago."

"That's fantastic news ... Here comes Blade Runner."

"Blade Runner?"

"Yeah, Ridley Scott's 1980s classic film about a detective tasked with hunting down rogue Replicants—artificial humans—who have come back to Earth from space colonies where they were enslaved."

"I get your point. In the near future, we might be chasing down runaway aged-care robots."

"Exactly."

"Perish the thought," she cautioned.

As Tula turned off Charlotte Pike Road onto Old Charlotte Pike, the lush farmland on either side of the narrow road came into view. Small farms with large homesteads dotted the landscape.

"Can we trust Cyrus Ram isn't leading us into a trap?" Tula asked, voicing a valid concern.

"We'll soon find out. To me, his concern for his daughter seemed genuine."

"I get that, but why would he put Wendy through all this if that were the case?"

I gazed out the window, the countryside passing in a verdant blur, pondering Tula's question. She had a point; Cyrus' actions seemed too extreme, especially considering his political aspirations. Finally, I admitted, "I can't explain it. People do irrational things ... I see it all the time in my game. Often, there's no logic to their actions or thoughts. The more I try to predict human behaviour, the more I'm proven wrong."

"I hear you ... Here we are," Tula said, slowing down to turn into a driveway that meandered through a densely wooded area.

"Okay, find a spot to park the car out of sight, and then we'll stake out the place."

Tula drove further along the driveway until the timber lodge came into view. She then veered off the road, steering the car into a copse of trees that effectively hid it from the lodge. We exited the car and cautiously made our way under cover until we reached the tree line, where we took positions with a clear view of the single-story timber lodge.

Positioned roughly fifty metres from the lodge, the ambiance around us was serene yet alive with nature's chorus. The setting sun filtered through the trees, creating a dance of flickering shadows around us. The croaking of frogs, the persistent chirping of crickets, and the sporadic rustle of a squirrel in the underbrush filled the air. The sight of the red Corvette parked under the carport was a silent confirmation that Johnny was indeed there. As the daylight waned, the approach of nightfall was palpable, with less than an hour of sunlight remaining.

"You don't think Cyrus or the Sheriff warned him about us, do you?" Tula asked.

"That would be counterproductive, increasing the risk to Wendy. Cyrus wouldn't want that. Plus, I think Johnny would've fled if he'd been tipped off."

"It looks pretty quiet in there."

"You married, Tula?"

"No, you?"

"Uh-uh, not that brave. You got a boyfriend?"

She hesitated before responding, "Detective Lois Pointer was my partner."

The realisation hit me unexpectedly. I hadn't seen it coming. It suddenly made perfect sense after she said it.

"Does the Sheriff know about you two...?"

"Hell no, he'd never condone that."

Just then, the front door of the lodge opened, and Johnny Ram stepped out. He was shirtless, showcasing a physique chiselled from years of bodybuilding, wearing only army green assault cargo pants.

"I reckon I could take him down with one shot," Tula whispered, her pistol aimed.

"I'm sure you could, Tonto, but we don't know who else is inside. He might have an accomplice."

"Tonto?" she queried, lowering her gun.

I chuckled, attempting to lighten the mood. "Just a joke. I think I told you, a friend of mine calls me kemosabe, and I call him Tonto, from the—"

"The Lone Ranger, I know. It was my Pop's favourite TV show."

"Once he goes back inside, I'll go get a closer look through the windows. We need to be sure Wendy's there."

After a few minutes, Johnny disappeared back inside.

"I think he knows we're here," I whispered to Tula.

"How can you tell?"

"Just a hunch … There's probably concealed CCTV in the trees along the driveway."

"What I can't figure out is why he would come here," Tula mused, her tone reflecting her confusion.

"That's bothering me too."

As the sun dipped below the horizon, the shadows around us deepened. I pulled out my phone and quickly adjusted the settings. "Switch your phone to vibrate … so I can call you. Cover me," I instructed Tula before drawing my pistol.

Taking a deep breath, I sprinted across the open field to the side of the lodge. The muffled sound of two male voices talking inside reached my ears. Peering cautiously through a side window, I spotted a burly man in a red and black plaid flannel shirt, seated on the arm of a lounge chair with a rifle across his lap, seemingly in conversation with someone I assumed was Johnny, identifiable by his army pants.

Needing a better view to confirm Wendy's presence, I edged under the carport towards the rear of the lodge, my back against the wooden façade. At the Corvette, I took out my Swiss Army knife and deflated its front tyre, then the rear, effectively immobilising the vehicle. Moving on, I reached the back of the lodge. A black Ford Pickup was parked further away, but finding Wendy was my priority. A quick glance through the rear kitchen window revealed it was empty. Just then, Johnny crossed the kitchen doorway, heading towards the living room. Sensing his urgency, I phoned Tula.

I whispered, "Tula, he's on the move. Two males inside, Wendy's whereabouts unknown..."

"He's coming out," Tula interrupted.

Johnny appeared on the front porch, clutching Wendy from behind, her mouth gagged, hands bound. He brandished a pistol at her head and shouted, "I know you're out there, we saw you come in. It's just two of you against two of us. Here's the deal. Arrange with my brother and Tanner for free passage out of Tennessee by car for me and my friend. I'll take Wendy with me, and once I'm clear, I'll drop her in a town. You know what'll happen if you don't agree. You've got an hour."

Tula quickly took a series of photos of Johnny with Wendy as evidence. Then said with a steady voice, "Axis, I think I can take him out."

"You sure? If you miss..."

"I can do it," she asserted, her determination clear.

I positioned myself against the back door. "On the count of three."

Tula slipped her phone into her top pocket and took aim. I counted down. "Three ... two ... one..."

A single shot rang out. Johnny went down.

"Run here, Wendy!" Tula yelled.

Reacting swiftly, I kicked open the back door and burst into the lodge. Inside, the other man, clearly startled, was heading towards the front door, rifle in hand. He swung around to aim at me, but I was ready. "Two against one, drop it!" I commanded forcefully.

He complied, lowering the rifle and slowly raising his hands in surrender. I cautiously approached him, keeping focused. "Hands behind you," I ordered firmly. Once he was securely handcuffed, I guided him to sit in an armchair before moving to the front porch.

There, Johnny's lifeless body lay, a bullet hole precisely in the centre of his forehead—a testament to Tula's sharpshooting skills from fifty metres away. Wendy, now safe, was with Tula, her expression a mix of relief and disbelief at the sudden turn of events. The danger was over, and Wendy was finally out of harm's way.

After the intense events at the lodge, we awaited the arrival of the police. As anticipated, they cordoned off the area, designating it a crime scene. They took comprehensive statements from Wendy and us, meticulously documenting the sequence of events. Once satisfied with the information we provided, they permitted us to depart.

Wendy, though physically unscathed, was understandably distraught by the ordeal. Despite her shaken state, she was open to discussing her experience. During our drive back to Nashville, she recounted her ordeal, offering insights that helped clarify the entire situation.

It emerged that Cowboy was the initial abductor, acting on Johnny Ram's orders. In debt to Johnny for a loan used to buy his car and band equipment, Cowboy, while not violent towards her, had been responsible for delivering her to Johnny's car yard. There, she was confined in a room. Only on the last day was she hastily moved to his ranch.

At the ranch, she overheard the gunfire exchange between Johnny, his accomplice Ritchie Burns, and the police. Following the shootout, she was quickly taken to the lodge. While there, she eavesdropped on a conversation between Johnny and Ritchie. Johnny was planning to coerce his brother Cyrus into arranging their escape to Florida.

Wendy's account during our return to Nashville shed light on the intricate motivations and actions of all involved. This not only illuminated the ordeal she had endured but also uncovered a deep-rooted conspiracy leading to the wrongful imprisonment of an innocent man. Her revelations were pivotal in comprehending the full extent of the events and the ensuing injustice.

CHAPTER
FIFTEEN

Charlie was engrossed in his work at his desk when Carol entered, disrupting his focus. "Serina Sun, Gerri Jewel, Kane Stevenson, and Lucian Grange are waiting in reception," she informed him.

Acknowledging her with a nod, Charlie soon welcomed the group into his office, guiding them to the lounge area. He handed out copies of the new agreement for their perusal.

Kane Stevenson was the first to share his views. "I've discussed the numbers with the studio, and they're on board. The real issue lies in the logistics of the treasure hunt."

"That aspect wasn't within my negotiating remit, Mr Stevenson. Such details should be coordinated directly with the Yan family."

A puzzled Stevenson added, "But isn't Niko currently in Hong Kong?"

Charlie, fingers thoughtfully positioned under his chin, calmly replied, "There's no definitive evidence linking Mr Yan's presence in Hong Kong to any such expedition."

"What if he is though?" Gerri chimed in, sounding slightly worried.

Charlie suggested practically, "Perhaps a direct conversation with him or an invitation to the studio for joint planning might alleviate these concerns. Serina, your thoughts?"

Serina hesitated briefly, exchanging glances with Grange before responding to Charlie. "I value your guidance, Charlie."

"And would you be interested in participating in such a planning session?" he inquired further.

Her answer came hesitantly. "I ... I'm not sure."

Grange confidently interjected, "She can defer that decision to me."

As the meeting wrapped up, Charlie stood and offered handshakes for farewells to everyone but Gerri.

Once alone with Charlie, Gerri approached him, her tone slightly suggestive. "Regarding last night, Charlie?"

Offering his hand, Charlie maintained a professional front. "It never happened, Gerri. Goodbye, and thank you."

She grasped his hand, masking disappointment with a smile. "Well, if you ever reconsider, Charlie Chan, you know where to find me."

"I'll bear that in mind," Charlie responded, his tone non-committal.

Exiting the meeting room, he stopped at Enzo perched on the edge of Carol's desk.

"So, how was the date? Are you two an item now?" Charlie asked casually.

Enzo, changing the subject, queried, "We're not going after the treasure, boss?"

Responding with his characteristic wit, Charlie quipped, "No, I've got to give birth before that can happen."

Enzo and Carol shared a look of bemusement, their expressions mirroring their mutual surprise at Charlie's unexpected remark.

~ ~ ~

After Tula dropped me off at the Conrad, she graciously offered to escort Wendy to reunite with Sherri and the others at Eo's ranch. I anticipated a tranquil evening with a satisfying meal and a soothing bath. However, a lengthy phone discussion with Patricia about the case's resolution meant foregoing the bath and heading straight to the sack.

The following morning, rejuvenated by a sound sleep, I received a call from Tula. We had an appointment at the Sheriff's office at 9 am. The day was splendid, and feeling refreshed, I opted to walk there.

Upon arrival, I found Tula in reception, donning her uniform again, though I had a preference for her in civilian attire. I was unsure of what to expect from Sheriff Tanner, particularly considering his questionable involvement with Cyrus Ram and their efforts to manipulate justice. The revelation of their actions could potentially devastate their careers.

This time, we were offered chairs in Tanner's office.

"I presume Wendy is safe?" he queried.

"Yes, sir," Tula confirmed.

"Why did you proceed without backup?" he probed.

"Cyrus Ram asked us not to put Wendy's life at undue risk," I replied.

"But you did," he countered.

"No, our operation was designed to safely extract her. Johnny Ram intended to use Wendy as leverage for his release," I clarified.

"How could you know that?" he pressed.

"I overheard his conversation with Ritchie Burns, his cohort," I disclosed.

Tanner then scrutinised Tula's actions, but I promptly defended her. "She neutralised Ram with a precise shot from fifty metres. Let's be frank, Sheriff. Certain individuals abused their power. This debacle could provoke lawsuits against Cyrus Ram and others. But that's not my concern now—my job here is done," I concluded, standing up and placing my badge on his desk. Without another word, I turned and walked out of the office.

Tula caught up with me outside. "Well said, Axis. Thank you for the support."

"Hey, you deserved it Kiddo. You took the shot ... I knew it wouldn't miss, it was for Lois, wasn't it?" I asked, noticing a hint of emotion in her eyes for the first time.

"Yes, it was," she acknowledged, her voice a blend of grief and determination. Suddenly, she embraced me warmly. "Thank you, Axis."

Two hours later, I was among a gathering of around thirty people at Brian X's graveside. The air was heavy with sombreness as the priest wrapped up his eulogy. Just then, a car arrived, and Ziggy Stardust, accompanied by the four girls, approached the grave. Ziggy's androgynous look sparked murmurs among the attendees.

Setting down a black box resembling a suitcase, Ziggy pressed a button, and unexpectedly, it played the intro of a song. Ziggy began to sing in a soulful elegy, his voice imbued with deep emotion.

My heart holds memories
I still recall

And when I'm lost at sea
They lead me to shore

I've never been on my own
But now I sail alone

Forever taking
The long way home

As days go drifting by
I reach out to you
But deep in my heart I know
Our love wasn't true

Was I just a stepping-stone
At war with the great unknown
Forever taking
The long way home

If I could catch the wind
Back to where I have been

I'd still be taking
The long way home

Floating in the ocean

A world of emotion

I'm all lost at sea

Can someone rescue me

And though I'm all alone
At war with the great unknown
I'll still be taking
The long way home

Forever taking
The long way home

The long way home

As the last notes of the song dwindled, a deep silence enveloped the crowd. The emotional depth of the song was palpable, moving many to tears. Eo's captivating voice, the resonant lyrics, and the gentle, soothing frequencies that Brian had uncovered combined to create a moving homage to Brian's memory. This instance surpassed mere grief; it stood as a tribute to the unifying force of music and its profound ability to touch the human soul.

This was more than a farewell; it was an affirmation of music's capacity to heal, connect, and transcend. In those few minutes, the song had not only honoured Brian's contributions but had also bound us all in a shared experience of loss and hope. It was a powerful reminder of how art, in its purest form, can transform and uplift, bridging gaps between hearts and minds.

Standing there, I realised I had witnessed something quite remarkable. Eo's performance, enhanced by the subliminal frequencies, had reached even the most sceptical and hardened among us. The music seemed to have a transformative effect, softening hard edges and dispelling bitterness.

In that instant, I harboured a hope, almost a yearning, for Eo to continue utilising this gift to impact and uplift more souls. His fusion of a mystical, hippie, peace-loving vibe with these transformative frequencies felt like a key to unlocking a more empathetic and united humanity, one liberated from the long-standing binds of anger, greed, and tyranny.

Reflecting on the prospect of such a positive force spreading globally, I couldn't help but feel a surge of optimism. Maybe, through the conduit of music and the right frequencies, we could indeed start to mend some of the deep-rooted wounds that have scarred the human psyche.

As the emotionally laden funeral drew to a close and the crowd began to thin, I navigated my way towards Eo and the girls. Sherri, with warmth in her eyes, embraced me. "Thank you for risking your life for Eo's and Wendy's."

Wendy approached, her arms open and tears glistening in her eyes. "I don't know how to thank you, Axis."

"Just remember, it was Detective Rita Suarez, a Choctaw Indian from Lauderdale County, whose birth name is Tula, meaning 'mountain peak', who saved your life," I gently reminded her.

Eo then joined our small gathering. "The loss of Brian and Detective Pointer was senseless. Thank you for everything, Axis."

Sherri, practical as ever, chimed in, "Please have Patricia send me your invoice."

Walking through the peaceful cemetery grounds towards the car park, I asked about their future plans. Sherri confirmed their dedication to the commune with a determined smile, acknowledging the recent events as a poignant reminder of its importance.

"It's unfortunate that the rifts with your father, and Wendy's with hers, remain unresolved," I commented.

"Only time can heal those wounds," Sherri responded, her voice tinged with a hint of resignation.

The drive to the airport with Tula was reflective, our conversation marked by the gravity of our recent trials. Our bond, though newly formed, felt deep and enduring. I sensed a spiritual connection to her ancient Indian roots, a bond that seemed destined to last.

"I think you and Patricia should visit my homeland someday. I'd love for you to meet my elders," Tula suggested.

"I'd like that," I responded, already anticipating the visit. "And I hope the robot works out for Lone Running Wolf."

~ ~ ~

Seated in business class on a Dreamliner, 39,000 feet in the air with a JD in hand, my thoughts drifted to Patricia and Kendy. I was eager to recount my experiences, especially about Eo and the Solfeggio frequencies Brian had identified in his voice and music. Pulling out my phone, I opened the selfie taken with Eo and the girls in the car park after the funeral. To my surprise, everyone was clear and focused, except for Eo. In his place was a mysterious, almost ethereal zigzag flash of light. Was it a mere camera anomaly or something more profound? Deep down, I sensed it was the latter, a subtle indication of Eo's extraordinary nature, leaving me pondering and curious.

Keep an eye out for:

Axis Stone Mysteries-Book 9

The song lyrics featured in 'The Ziggy Stardust Dead Ringer' are with the consent of Keadybros music publishing

http://www.keadybros.com

'WALRUS DREAMS'

(Gary L. Keady and John M. Vallins)
Copyright©1996. Keady/Vallins
Performed by: World

'LONG WAY HOME'

(Gary L. Keady and John M. Vallins)
Copyright©2012. Keady/Vallins
Performed by: World

Visit

http://www.bigislandpublishing.au